HER SECRET CRUSH

HER SECRET CRUSH

JOLIE MOORE

MOORE DIGITAL
MEDIA INC

This edition published by
Moore Digital Media Inc
1125 N Fairfax Ave
West Hollywood CA 90046

Cover Designer: Croco Designs

eISBN: 978-1-64414-004-8
ISBN: 978-1-64414-035-2

Also by Jolie Moore

What Was Perfect

What Was Lost

What Was True

Taming the Bad Boy

Fifty First Dates

Chapter One

SABRINA

THE SOUND of heavy breathing filled the room. Not breathing like someone was hiking up a steep hill. It was *sex* breathing.

A breath was sucked in. Came out in a high-pitched panting.

Then a woman moaned in apparent pleasure.

I opened my eyes, got blinded by the sun. Closed them.

For fuck's sake, my neighbors were at it again. They believed in an open-windows policy. I didn't think anyone needed that much fresh air and I was from Canada where fresh air was a thing.

"Allen, oh God, oh, oh." Maribel's voice spiraled higher and higher one octave at a time.

"I'm gonna do you so hard," Allen huffed.

"Do it, oh, oh oh!" Maribel's voice had gone from alto to soprano in a few breathless heartbeats.

Every time Allen thrust, she moaned. Every time Maribel moaned, he groaned. Then I got that tingly feeling between my legs and I grabbed the duvet and hauled it and the blanket and sheet over my head as if I was going to somehow block out sex sounds and get right back to sleep. I'd seen the clock. I knew better.

Despite my best efforts to ignore it, I'd seen the glowing clock. It was eight and I should have been out on the trail with Spencer, training for Kilimanjaro like a good L.A. transplant. Squirming out of my mummy-like duvet, I poked my head out enough to see, then my arm swung out to slip open my side table drawer. Let me tell you with my own window open that fresh air was hella cold.

Not letting too much cold seep in under the covers, in less than a minute I'd snatched my vibrator under the blanket with me and was going to town piggybacking off the neighbors' orgasm. Images of Maribel and Allen faded replaced by a certain store clerk with biceps I wanted to lick, when I rolled over on the remote control and my TV snapped on. Blue light filled the darkened room. When my eyes adjusted, I saw it.

The spray of sparkling diamonds flying through the air then landing on wet cobblestones caught my eye.

My mind came to a screeching halt like my little Mazda did when I came within sight of a Beverly Hills red light camera. Talk about going from buzz to buzkill.

Actually, I was going from buzzkill to *The Buzz*.

"Fuck it," I cried out frustrated in more ways than one. I looked around the room as if my mom would pop out of the shadows and condemn my cursing. But there was no one here but me. It was a mighty big display for a Canadian. We were a polite bunch. If anyone asked, I'd blame it all on the influence of living south of the border.

My vibrator hit the carpeted floor with a thud. I really hoped the damn thing was sturdy enough to survive. Good ones weren't cheap. I'd already spent a bunch of money on the bad ones. Then I lifted the remote and unmuted the set. That five-second clip of cascading diamonds was becoming my favorite form of self-torture.

After a commercial that promised I'd frolic through daisies if I ate a particular brand of yogurt, a claim that I knew from personal experience was patently false, the CBT morning entertainment news show, *The Buzz*, came back on the air, the show's trumpet-heavy theme blaring.

In true *Buzz* fashion, the roundtable of three—a guy in horn-rimmed glasses and a bow tie, a former beauty queen, and an ex-professional football player—played the clip three different times.

Like he was diagramming a play, the football star drew white lines all over stilled video photos.

"The exes are for each diamond unleashed. No touchdown here, folks. Gemma Hart fumbled." On cue, the audience groaned like the movie star had dropped a game-winning ball.

Not to be outdone, the host in tortoiseshell horn-rims, cleared the screen and took over the stylus. He drew a single line from her mouth to a speech bubble, talking as he wrote.

"I hope this makes you forget about my sex tape," appeared to come from the movie star's mouth.

In an effort to calm that awful sinking feeling in the pit of my stomach I'd come to associate with that ten-second video clip, I looked down, squinted my eyes, and made the bed and sorted through my drawers for exercise clothes all the while ignoring the beauty queen's high-pitched rant.

In a second of silence I glanced back at the television screen to see the three laughing riotously. Even all alone in my house some five miles from the TV studio, I could feel their condemnation weighing on my shoulders like twin boulders. Then it swirled over me like ocean waves had the one time I'd tried and failed at surfing. Either way this whole incident made me feel like I was drowning and deserved it.

Though I felt really awful for Gemma Hart, having ruined the former recluse's first step back into the spotlight, I was selfishly thankful my jewelry design business, Severn Gael, hadn't been mentioned—*this time.*

Mysterious connections from my neighbor and friend, Mona Love, had gotten me the commission to design for Gemma. What should have been the high point of my career had gone terribly, terribly wrong.

When I opened up my eyes fully and looked up again, they were still at it. Gemma walked back and forth on the London street like someone in the control booth was moving their fingers from rewind to fast-forward and back again. Must be the world's slowest entertainment news day. God, this was awful, watching each one of the hosts vying for one-upmanship via snark.

When the next commercial blared, I snapped off the set. My usual habit of leaving the TV on low, images flickering and rumbling voices keeping me company throughout the day as I moved through my house that was also my studio, wasn't going to happen. Not today. Maybe not for a lot of days, until *The Buzz* and all its companions found another story to glom onto. Surely one of the Kardashians was due for attention. One of them had to be having a baby, launching a clothing line, or getting married and divorced.

I jogged downstairs where my dog Spencer was waiting patiently by the back door. While I let him out, mindlessly watching him lift his leg along the property's perimeter, my mind went right back to the clip *The Buzz* had shown. It had been last month's debut of recluse star Gemma Hart, coming out of years of hiding to star in a West End London play. Most celebs would have been out of the news by now. But with her decade-old sex tape out there, the tabloids would never leave Gemma be.

In video and in still, I'd seen it too many times to count. Gemma Hart had worn a diamond choker that branched across the star's neck in delicate curlicues. I had been supremely proud of my latest creation—until Gemma had lifted her hand and craned her neck to wave at a child in a wheelchair. Because of course all the cameras were focused on her then. Celebrities and the disabled were money shots.

Then...BAM.

Jewelry malfunction.

Seventy-five thousand dollars' worth of diamonds all over London's dark, damp pavement. It was always followed by a smash cut to a grainy photo of Gemma in bed with perennial rehab patient and top-grossing Hollywood actor Drew O'Bryan.

Gemma's hunky-looking fiancé had been quick enough to recover all but one of the stones. The last diamond was long lost under the tires of a mini cab or in the pocket of one lucky bystander.

After that, my phone had been ringing off the hook, but not for orders from Severn Gael, but tabloids calling for interviews asking if I'd staged the stunt on purpose. As if...

In quick succession, the humiliating moment was covered by *TMZ, Entertainment Tonight,* and *E! News.* Not to mention *The Buzz,* vaulting Gemma to the top of this year's worst-dressed list in the show's last week's year-end round up.

Memories of Gemma Hart's humiliation during her first public appearance in a decade making my hands unsteady, I whistled for my one guaranteed source of comfort in the house, Spencer. Canine loyalty had to be the best balm there was. Satisfied that his perimeter search hadn't turned up any evidence of foul play or lizards, he loped in, drank from his water bowl, then sat at my feet. I knelt down to rub one of his soft ears between my fingers. The dog groaned in pleasure.

Good for him, I thought. Dogs were hedonistic beings. They knew how to take pleasure, and how to enjoy themselves. I could take a lesson or two from Spencer.

I wasn't thinking about anything but the dog and how much he enjoyed rolling through grass or picking up balls when I stood without a thought and hit my head against one of the low beams. The pain that exploded from the crown of my head as it hit one of the fat ceiling beams made all thoughts of public embarrassment or pleasure flee from my mind.

Damn...so much better than my earlier swear words...

I rubbed at the sore spot, relieved that there was no blood on my fingers when I pulled away. Five years I'd been in this house, and I still did that at least once a week. When I'd bought the house, the real estate agent had described the exposed ceiling beams as a lovely feature. What it added up to was a lot of space that wasn't exactly usable. Whether that was charming, special, or just a total square footage fraud was open to interpretation.

The John Malkovich house is how she thought of it, from the eponymous movie with its low-ceilinged seven and a half floors. The previous owner had daughters, and the little preschoolers had their dolls in miniature houses and toys tucked in every little low ceiling corner. I hadn't planned to use any of that space, not being under four feet tall. Then I'd moved my studio space home to save money and build my business and now I wished I was four feet tall.

In my peripheral vision, something small and shiny

caught my eye. Was it the feather of a bird or a hairless rodent tail? The first I could tolerate and worry about later. The second made my skin crawl.

To the dog, I said, "If you brought me a gift that escaped and is breeding in my walls, speak now."

Spencer eyed me, then the tiny door I'd always thought was for plumbing or crawl space access, then me again, but remained silent.

A shudder ran through me, lifting the hair on the back of my neck and raising gooseflesh on my arms. Fearing mice or bats or pigeons swooping into the house, then needing to be relocated, I crouched and approached the door stealthily, taking care not to disturb any vermin likely making a home. I took a deep breath, summoning all my courage.

Now, on hands and knees, I crawled to the edge of the room and felt around where the wood met trim and plaster and hinges, hoping a long, hairless tail didn't slip through my fingers.

I paused.

I didn't need this.

I needed a lot of things.

Journalists with memory loss.

A good vibrator.

A better boyfriend.

Maybe shutting the door and leaving whatever it was to starve to death would solve the problem. I shook my head. The scratch of nails above my head at night or the potential smell of death lingering in the walls moved me closer to the little door.

For a long second, I craned my head over my shoulder, looking for the gloves I used to keep my hands free of cuts when I was snipping metal or shaving stones. Nah. Hands were washable, where the well-fitting leather gloves weren't, and I didn't want cooties contaminating them.

Fu...dge it. I pulled up my big girl panties and thrust my fingers toward the shadowy object. It wasn't slimy or scaly, thank goodness.

Instead my hands landed on something small, both rough and smooth at the same time. Bringing it out into the bright sunlight pouring down from the four roof skylights, I peered at it.

WTF? That "F" was for fudge, by the way in case any Canadians or moms thought otherwise.

A cameo? Did my hand just walk back in time a freaking hundred years? There was no way that wasn't really creepy.

Chapter Two

HENRY

I'D WALKED AS SLOWLY as I could. Nothing I could be doing could be called hiking. At least two different people had stopped me along the trail and asked if I needed help. *As if*, I'd wanted to say to the man in a visor who had to be otder than Methuselah or the woman who looked like she was fifteen seconds from giving birth.

Whenever I'd been in Los Angeles, I'd hiked this same trail with my dog Sadie. It was weird how doing nothing was the same without my dog. Instead of people asking me about going slow, they'd have been asking to pet Sadie, or about her breed, or temperament. That was one thing that was hard about this.

The other? I'd kind of been hoping just a little bit to run into Sabrina Lynch. Under duress, I'd probably admit to a low-level crush on her for quite some time, even though I'd never asked her out. It didn't seem fair to ask her for dinner one day, then travel out of town the next.

At least I knew her name. Otherwise my plan to run into her and ask her out would have been weird. Maybe not skeevy L.A. guy weird, but weird for me.

She was usually out by eight o'clock. Eight thirty at the latest. My phone said it was past nine and I was walking slow enough that snails were lapping me. I spied a bench and decided to sit. I slipped my sunglasses down so I could watch without looking like I was watching. I kicked the toes of my hiking shoes in the sand along the ridge of the Santa Monica Mountains thinking back to the time I'd finally learned Sabrina's name.

"Hey, Henry," I'd said, extending my hand and introducing myself, hoping the forwardness worked for me like it did for my naturally gregarious father.

Sabrina had dropped the half-dozen egg container in the hand basket and shook mine firmly with her now free hand.

"Had a craving for quiche, but was missing eggs. And without eggs..."

"No quiche," I finished. "Don't worry, you're in the right place. You've got the Rhodesian ridgeback, right?"

Her previously neutral face broke out into a big smile. "Spencer, yeah. Adopted him from a shelter. Can you believe he'd been there six months? Don't know why someone didn't take him home earlier. He's the nicest dog ever."

"Big dogs make people nervous." I shrugged, trying for nonchalance. Doing the "real men aren't afraid of large breeds" thing. "What are you putting in your quiche?" I asked in an attempt to keep the conversation going. She had a nice voice. I wanted to hear more of it, see that smile again.

"Leftovers, kind of like my mom does, ham, cheese, a bit of veg."

"Sounds good."

"Yeah, have you got cream? Now that I'm here, I'm nervous I might not have enough."

One of the old-timers was quietly hovering near the register, so I couldn't guide her around the store like I wanted to. I'd done my most gracious smile at the longtime customer.

"In the dairy case, behind the almond milk and non-dairy creamer."

And instead of getting a little one-on-one, I'd pointed. It was a country store not a mega mart. I manned the only register. She'd be back in a couple of minutes. By that time the other customer would hopefully be long gone.

With a small wave, she went off to the back corner of the store. For my other customer, I handed over a pack of cigarettes as well as a packet of nicotine gum, all stuff we kept behind the register. It took a lot for me to hold my tongue on the guy's lack of sense of irony and take the cash.

Rattan basket in hand, Sabrina was next at the register. I was never so glad that my parents were at a doctor's appointment, otherwise it would have been my dad charming her. A lot of people couldn't see past my dad's friendly bluster to the guy behind him.

"Do you drink wine?" I asked, because God knew

almost everyone in L.A. was abstaining from something. Alcohol and its companion, carbs, were often at the top of that list.

When she said, "I do," I came from behind the register again. She smelled sweet, like a mixture of lavender and vanilla. I could get used to that smell.

"Do you have a preference or favorite?" I'd asked like I'd been trained. Just because some thousand-dollar one-hundred-point wine was supposedly perfect, it was best to match the wine with the taste.

Her mouth ticked up in a half smile like she was embarrassed at her taste. "Not too sweet, why?"

"Leave your basket. I have an idea."

I took her back to the small corner shelf my parents had reluctantly given up to my efforts. From the European section, considerably smaller than the California one, I selected a green bottle with a fancy scripted label.

"This is a 2009 Marcel Deiss Rotenberg. It's a blend of Riesling and Pinot Gris. Stands up well to strong flavors like leek or lardons or cheese."

Subtly, the curvy blonde licked her lips as if imagining a feast. I'd have loved to have been an invited guest. Store clerks, though, didn't do that.

She wavered for a moment, then her smile got bigger. "Why not? This will make lunch more interesting. Maybe I'll try my new table."

"You just move here?" I was fishing. Maybe I'd be the one to show her around the city where I was born.

"No. OSH had one of those no-tax weekends, so I

saved nine percent on a table and chairs for the patio. It's nice eating outside. I'm trying to do it more often." I ate outside more when I lived in BC. So there's no reason not to eat out in a place with nearly perfect weather."

"It is nice eating outside. I usually eat lunch out there with Sadie." I gestured toward the little porch off the market.

"What is she?"

"A dog?"

We shared a laugh at my stupid joke. I liked it a lot that I could make her pretty smile wider.

"Breed?" It had been her real question when I'd gone for the obvious joke.

"Shepherd mix, maybe? Heinz fifty-seven, definitely."

"Is she made of ketchup?" Her eyebrows said she didn't get that joke.

"No, it's just a silly thing that means she's a mix of a zillion different breeds."

"She seems sweet no matter what she is."

"Let me get this rung up for you," I said, trying to work up the courage to go from eggs to cream to wine to coffee date.

I rang up her purchases, bagging as I went, gratified that it looked like she was cooking for one, a possible sign that she was single.

"Sixty-three, fifty-seven," I announced.

She opened her wallet, frowning when there appeared to be no more than a twenty in it.

"Damn. I only brought enough cash for the eggs."

"We take credit and debit." Just because we were small, didn't mean we weren't in tune with the global economy that seemed, these days, to work on plastic. That exact argument had finally worked on my parents, one of my best business decisions yet. I'd get them on board with the wine soon enough, and if not, well, I had other plans.

"Right, sure." She worked slim fingers with neat, short nails into one of the wallet's pockets. She handed over a gold card. "Here you go."

Sabrina Lynch glinted from the card. I memorized her name before sliding it through the register's card reader. I pointed to the terminal affixed to the wooden counter.

"Pin, please."

She carefully tapped in the four-digit number.

"Thanks so much for the wine. I wouldn't have had the courage to forage through that shelf on my own."

I tried not to blush at the compliment. There hadn't been much opportunity to use my hard-won knowledge, but this made me glad I'd suffered through the grueling sommelier classes. I was one giant step away from the Master designation and a future making lots more people happy by sending them home with wines they loved.

After that afternoon, I'd vowed to work up the courage to ask her out. It wasn't every woman who wanted to date a store clerk. Lawyers, doctors, and producers, sure, actors, absolutely, but regular Joes, not so much. Something told me Sabrina was different. But then Sadie had gotten sick and thoughts of wine, women, dating hadn't seemed important at all.

I'd found my dog coughing after our regular morning walk, and then hours later pacing around her dog bed after turning off my bedside lamp.

One vet trip for eleven-year-old Sadie had turned into a weeklong trial that had ended with the hardest decision I'd had to make in as many years.

Then I'd been back on the road visiting vineyards and studying and I'd had to tuck Sabrina in the back of my mind.

I looked up and down the hill again and thought I'd caught a flash of wavy blond hair and a dog pulling ahead. I stood and took in a deep breath of cool winter air and smog. It was time to run into Sabrina. My sommelier training was all done. In just a couple of months, if all went as planned, I'd have my own wine store in West Holly-wood. I'd be able to invite Sabrina back for after-hours wine tasting and...and well whatever came after that. I just had to convince one woman and her dog to give me a chance.

Chapter Three

SABRINA

I TURNED the cameo over in my palm. The craftsmanship on these old pieces was the bomb. A world away from the mass-marketed stuff called jewelry they sold in a spinning rack in every store. I'd seen jewelry in a housewares store last week. Curtains, candles, and a charm bracelet. Now there was an image I'd never scrub from my mind.

Sitting back on my haunches, I smoothed my work-roughened thumb over the face. Probably ivory. To my eye, the black stone looked to be jet. Turning over the silver case holding the contrasting materials, I tried to read tiny writing on the back.

Damn, I was only twenty-nine and couldn't read this. Any more years in this business and I'd be blind.

I tiptoed up the steps to the main area of my studio, careful not to hit my head on the beams up here that were even lower nor did I drop the piece. I laid the cameo on my worktable and pulled the powerful magnifying glass over it. Five lines were inscribed in beautiful calligraphy.

> *Love has this jet to which she clings*
> *With ivory and circling locks about*
> *Bone within silver to cast fear out*
> *Love once found has need of no such thing*
> *Set it free on a pair of dauntless wings*

What in ever-loving hell did all that mean? Art had been my favorite class in high school, not English poetry. The engraving was elaborate, and just varied enough that it must have been done by hand. Until last month I'd thought I'd become a skilled metal worker, but the level of detail on this cameo suggested some kind of amazing craftsman was behind it. It was sad that such an extraordinary piece should be lost. There was probably some family pining for the heirloom. For a fleeting moment I wondered how in the heck I'd find the owner.

Up here Allen and Maribel were even louder, but they were at their big finale. Allen ran a gallery that opened at eleven and he was never late. But I was by a good two hours.

Damn. *The Buzz*, Gemma Hart, and the cameo had conspired to throw me off track.

A creature of habit, the dog made his way down the stairs. The neighbors were our cue. Time for our daily hike even if it was a bit late.

The moment I lifted the leash from its place on the peg

by the door, the dog went blurry with his wiggling. Spencer spun around and around near the front door.

"You're making it nearly impossible to hook the leash."

Spencer perked one ear and spun more and more slowly until he settled into a sitting position.

"See, I've always known you understood English even though you pretend to misunderstand the words 'no digging' and 'no squirrels,' and 'no couch.'" I hooked six feet of leather onto his collar the moment he was still. It would be a good while before he could do the out-of-control spin again.

"Now we can go." Donning my sneakers, and a hat against the December cold, I opened and closed the front door and gate, jiggling the lock for security. Turning left, I made my way down the short bit of street before the hiking trail only feet from my home.

This was it.

This was the reason I put up with the three-and-a-half-foot loft ceilings and the too-close neighbors for this Los Angeles gem, only steps away, Franklin Canyon Park.

I passed all the rail-thin hikers, who promptly moved as far away as possible when Spencer and I came walking. It drove me nuts that every Angeleno thought a dog over fifty pounds was a pit bull. Spencer couldn't have been nicer. An attack-worthy guard dog he was not.

I blotted out everyone and worked through an intricate ring design I was trying to get just right for one of my favorite customers. When Spencer started to pull, I looked up.

Ah, it was Henry.

Spencer did a spin as a shiver shimmied up my spine. Gooseflesh raised under my sweater. My nipples got all hard and pointy. None of that was from the Los Angeles winter. It was all the tall hot guy filling my vision.

I'll admit to a mini crush on Henry since the first time I'd seen him. Who wouldn't, with his dark reddish hair and awesome arms that looked like he lifted lots of things. The last few times I'd worked up the nerve to talk to him, he'd always disappear for weeks or months at a time. If I was a little more insecure, I'd think I had some kind of cooties that had infected him.

He was here now, though. Right in front of my very eyes. My heart kicked up a notch and my sweaty palms nearly lost their grip on the leash. 'Cause there was nothing sexier than a clumsy chick.

The tall auburn-haired hiker never moved over. He wasn't afraid of my baby. I tried not to drool as I took in his beefy arms. Henry had gotten those nice biceps working at Canyon Country Mart, the deli/convenience store up at the top of the hill in that little shopping center on Mulholland.

Even though there were cheaper big box stores, I made a special detour to Corey's Discount Pet in the same center, and always smiled when I saw Henry's dog sunning itself outside. He'd often prop a little umbrella over the one tiny spot of grass so Sadie could relax in comfort.

Today, Henry was walking a bit slower than usual.

Maybe this was my chance to say more than "hi" and "nice dog" or "great weather."

The last time I'd even dared say something had been by far my absolute worst opening gambit. I'd been buying last-minute supplies for cookies I was bringing to a party and Henry had been standing near the register, smiling.

He'd been wearing a number 72 basketball jersey. First-round draft pick, Maximo Lara, had picked the number because it was the average temperature in Los Angeles.

"Got everything you need?" he'd asked with a smile. That mouth with its perfect lips and touchable scruff did funny things to my belly. The broad, muscular shoulders on display had tied my tongue in knots for the hundredth time.

"Yeah. Great weather we're having." Those were all the words I could manage to put together that didn't sound like gibberish.

He'd looked at me like I was daft in the head. Because if one thing was true about Los Angeles, it was that it was nearly always great weather and I'd stated the obvious. The only thing I could think of that would be worse is I'd said "the sky is blue," or "you must like Maximo Lara."

After that, I'd stuck to talking to his dad. The smiles Henry had sent my way on subsequent visits were...sympathetic.

So when I saw him on this blustery Wednesday, I was all prepared to duck my head and look the other way. Save my quick mental snapshot of him in his dark green tee for the days when I needed a fantasy boyfriend to lift my spirits or combat the sounds of my neighbors.

Usually he'd be walking his dog down, as I'd be walking my dog up. Then Spencer and I would pass him going the other way and that would be it—another missed opportunity. I figured one day he'd find a nice girl, a thinner, prettier one without a nine-inch scar in the middle of her chest and he'd go in the forever fantasy pile with all the other guys I hadn't had the guts to get to know.

Today, Henry snapped me out of my self-imposed funk because something was different. He was walking in the same direction. Maybe the late bird caught a worm too. My heart sped up because today I would get at least a good ten or twenty minutes to fill up on the sight of him.

I tried to slow down the heartbeat that sped up a little every time I saw Henry. I needed to think, not think about my heart. Sometimes I could swear I heard my artificial valve clicking when I got excited.

There was so much I wanted to know about him. Was he single was my biggest question. Not that I'd ever have the courage to ask a guy like him out. Hot guys with perfectly broad shoulders that filled the hell out of a plaid flannel and just the right amount of scruff didn't go for women like me.

Women with calloused fingers, and nine-inch scars bisecting their chest, and less than a stick-thin figure. Well, not never. I'd been a hell of a catch in my small British Columbia town where single loggers and oil riggers outnumbered single women. There wasn't a weekend when I hadn't had a date.

But not in Los Angeles, where a single guy could throw a pebble in any direction and hit a beautifully turned-out actress. I'd already passed one not five seconds ago. A woman who was on TV every Tuesday pretending to be a pediatrician. The woman had been blonder and thinner and even better looking than on the small screen.

I tried to watch Henry without looking like I was ogling him like a stalker. Then I looked again, longer this time, because something wasn't right. Ah, he didn't have his dog. I scanned the area because Sadie had been tan like the ground and rocks in the park. There was no off-leash Sadie running around, though. He didn't even have the bright pink leash he usually carried.

Henry was alone.

Damn. Alone wasn't good. The last time I'd seen his dog, Sadie's muzzle had been gray. The dog had also had a slight limp marring her usual sunny disposition. There was only one conclusion I could draw from that and it wasn't a happy ending.

I warned myself sternly, if I said anything at all to Henry, it wouldn't be about his dog.

The dusty path narrowed, putting us less than three feet from each other. I gathered up my courage because it suddenly occurred to me that the worst that could happen is he blew me off. I'd still have my fantasies, though.

"Hi," I stuttered. Oh okay, I was as tongue-tied as before. So much for screwing up courage.

Great, I sounded like an idiot.

The auburn hair I could see curling from under his knit cap was slightly damp with sweat. He'd likely already covered a couple of miles. From passing by him in my car some days, I knew he walked all the way from the store to the bottom and back, not driving to the head of the trail like most L.A. hikers.

"Hey yourself," he said. Well it wasn't a marriage proposal, but it wasn't a blow-off either. He stopped for a long second to take a deep drink from the Nalgene bottle unclipped from the belt loop of his cargo pants. Spencer did his spinning thing near the man, looking up at Henry in frank admiration.

Men.

Given the slightest encouragement, my pup would be offering his belly for rubbing. I tugged lightly on the leash just to make sure my dog didn't totally sell me out.

Unfortunately, my dog did not have a lick of sense when it came to logic. Somehow, Spencer had wound the leather through Henry's legs.

One minute we humans were both upright while I frantically tried to untangle the dog, in the next, all three of us were on the ground in one big heap.

"Oh gosh! So sorry," I gasped as Henry's weight settled on my body.

Sorry?

That was an abject lie. I was not in the least bit sorry. He felt as good on top of me as I'd imagined in the dark of night, when I'd been alone with my thoughts and my electric magic wand.

Spencer quickly righted himself and tried to pull out of our little mammal sandwich, jerking his leash and winding us ever tighter together.

"Wow, I didn't see that coming," Henry huffed, his lips only inches from mine. It wasn't the only body part that lined up perfectly.

"Spencer got excited," I said. My dog wasn't the only one. It had been some time since I'd been with someone who wasn't a figment of my imagination, and Henry's hard body was doing all sorts of exciting and prickly things to mine.

"I'm sorry if I'm crushing you." Henry shifted, and I went from low-grade tingling to full-on arousal.

"Let me." I wiggled until I could reach the clasp. With a jerk of my thumb, I was able to release Spencer.

Immediately, unfortunately, the pressure eased.

"This is twisted everywhere." His deep voice rumbled first through his body then mine. I prayed that he couldn't feel my nipples poking through my bra and sweater. It was as I'd suspected all along. He lit me up like a Christmas tree. 'Twas the right season.

"Ah, my leg," I said, blood flowing below the ankle again.

"And my boot laces," he replied.

In less than a minute, Henry's strong, capable hands made quick work of unwinding the leather leash from first my calves, then his. He stood, then stretched his arm toward me. I took his hand. With a gentle tug, I fell into him. He was even stronger than he looked. My palms hit solid muscle his shirt did little to disguise. Touching him was like fire. I stepped back quickly, keeping my balance this time.

"Spencer!"

The dog came back from sniffing the bushes with a trot, not a care in the world for what he'd done a moment ago.

Henry gave a quick laugh. There was a little crinkle at the corners of his blue eyes, but the smile didn't reach his lips.

Those eyes.

The swirl of emotion reached out and grabbed at my heart. It made me forget the one thing I wasn't supposed to ask.

"Where's *your* dog?" I blurted.

The second the words were out of my mouth, I regretted all three of them.

Broad shoulders slumped. I immediately wanted to stuff that question right back in. Not only was I careless with diamonds, but tact as well. I'd been out of Canada too damned long.

"She died last week," he murmured.

Kneeling down in the gritty yellow sand, I unwound the twists from Spencer's leash. The position made it easy to avoid Henry's eyes. Thinking of dogs I'd lost, and the possibility of losing Spencer, put a big old frog in my throat. I titled my head back to swallow Kermit. It must have been the strong winter sun that made my eyes water.

"I'm really sorry. I know how awful this can be," I offered in condolence.

Henry extended a hand. Ignoring the tingle at our touch, I grasped it hard and let him bring me to my feet again, keeping my balance this time.

He swallowed deeply, his Adam's apple bobbing gently. "Thank you for saying that."

"For...? Only a heartless soul wouldn't be sad for you. Everyone's been through it." I'd gone from hot and bothered to cold and sad in a matter of seconds. I had to start moving, trying to shake off the inevitability, the anguish of loss.

Without invitation, Henry walked with us. Fortunately for my sanity, he was a safe distance away on the other side of the dog.

"I'm kind of pretending in my head that Spencer is going to live forever," I said, picking one elephant over another.

Henry looked at me for a moment, then turned away. Winter sun had made his eyes smart like mine. For five minutes, they hiked together in silence.

When he turned back to me, he was composed.

Breaking the silence, he said, "Where'd you get that hat?"

I touched the top of my head. Yep, I was wearing a hand-knit cap. Had I known Henry was going to be here with me, I'd have done something to untangle my too-long, too-wiry waves. Like get a four-hundred-dollar Beverly Hills haircut I couldn't afford.

I needed a new head shot anyway. One that made me look as different as possible from the one that had appeared next to the frozen action shot of Gemma Hart, hand at throat, red lips in an "O" of astonishment, diamonds caught in midair.

Ugh.

I hated that my mind went right to the damned jewelry all the time now. It was like pulling the bandage off a wound every damn time I thought of it. I glanced over and Henry was looking at me, expectantly, waiting for an answer.

Right. The hat.

"My mom knitted it. It's one of her empty-nest hobbies, I think."

"Cute. She did a good job. It suits you."

Cute. Had he just called my mom's beige hat cute? Was it possible he thought that *I* was cute? I tried not to smile too big. Instead, I checked my watch.

Damn, not only was I late today, I was slow as well. I stepped up my pace. Training actually involved, well, training. I looked around at the few other hikers. Not a one was wearing a knit cap like me and Henry. Maybe it was some kind of fate, kismet.

"Did your mom knit your hat?" Maybe they had that in common, too.

His laugh was small. But there was that sexy crinkle

around the eyes again, the earlier sadness gone. I liked this smiling, sexy Henry.

"My mom is probably back at the store balancing the books. That'll be the longest she'll probably sit still today. Needle work or knitting...can't see her doing it."

"Your mom works there? I've only seen your dad." I hoped that didn't sound too stalkerish. I did go to the pet store up on the hill. It wasn't like I made that drive to the store farthest from my house *only* to see Henry.

Corey's Discount Pet had the natural food that the vet had recommended for Spencer. If I happened to take a long look at the goings on at Canyon Country Mart, hoping to catch a glimpse of Henry, it was only coincidence.

"He's a very friendly guy. My mom is kind of the opposite, she's not a people person. Really shy, actually."

"But she works at the store?" I asked, trying to remember if I'd ever seen an older woman at the market.

"Always in the back unless something happens to bring her out front."

"I like your dad."

Chester Barnhill was a barrel-chested, gregarious guy who introduced himself and shook the hand of everyone he met. Always ready with a suggestion of a new food or drink.

He'd gotten me addicted—for a good six months—to seasoned taco shells that only his store carried.

Come to think of it, Henry hadn't been around much during that time. After coming weekly, I'd finally worked up the courage to ask him out, then like every time before, he'd disappeared.

The smartwatch on my arm beeped. I made the next hundred steps on my toes.

"Whoa, you're moving fast," Henry said. He looked down at my awkwardly placed feet. "And hopping? On your toes?"

"Training," I puffed between breaths.

"You going to do the marathon in March? On your toes?"

"Running? Me? No," I retorted. "I'm the opposite of lithe running girl. I'm more the enjoys-baking-cookies-and-eating-them girl."

"Are you an actress auditioning for one of the roles where you have to be hyper thin?"

"That's sweet of you, but no. Not an actress." That job was for pretty girls, not sturdy girls.

"Then you're more than fine. At least I think so. Los Angeles could use more real women like you."

My heart did a little flutter. Real women. He wasn't a model chaser. Maybe I had a chance. Did I want a chance? Geez. It was easier having a five-minute fantasy about him every so often. The real him was a lot all at once.

"So what are you training for?" he asked. He wasn't having any problem keeping up with her. But of course not, he hiked twice as far every day.

"I'm planning on climbing Mount Kilimanjaro," I admitted. The first people I'd told were my parents. And they were biting their nails, worried I'd drop dead on the side of an African mountain. I hadn't had the guts to tell more than a couple of my friends, worried that people would laugh at my lifelong dream, the timetable for which had moved up considerably after Gemma's premiere. I needed time away from the disapproving internet trolls.

"Seriously? Wow."

"Yeah, that's everyone's response. It's my present to myself for my thirtieth birthday."

Now that I'd revealed my lack of confidence in my weight *and* my age, I didn't know what in the heck else to say. One day I was going to be a lot less Canadian. We were an entirely too honest and forthcoming bunch. I wanted to be more like the tight-lipped Americans who never said what they meant except when swearing. That part, I had down to a fine art.

"It's not your average vacation plan. It's not the Paris marathon or riding a gondola down the Venice canals," he said. "Where is Kilimanjaro, anyway? Africa somewhere?"

"Tanzania, to be exact. I'm thinking of doing a safari afterwards."

"Wow, that's huge. How long will all that take?"

"A week to acclimate to the altitude. A week to climb. Then a week to do a safari afterwards."

"You leaving soon?" he asked, as if he were genuinely interested and not just shooting the breeze.

I threw back my head and laughed. "No. I just started the eight-week training program a few days ago. But I'm giving myself five months to get in shape. If Spencer and I survive through March, then I'll buy the tickets."

"That's good to hear."

"Why?"

"Because I'd like to take you on a date. Maybe try dinner."

"Sure, that would be cool," I said, trying to *sound* cool, but failing miserably. God, did I sound eager? Like I didn't have a clue in my head about how to play the dating game. It was a game, wasn't it? That's what my last boyfriend had said. It was like poker, and I'd sorely lost time and again. He'd said I didn't have guile or whatever it was I needed to make a relationship exciting.

"What's this eight-week regime?"

For the next couple of kilometers, I told him about all the hiking, walking, and weight workout I was supposed to do.

All too quickly, we were at the summit. The breathtaking view didn't hold my attention like it usually did.

"Can see out to the Pacific today," Henry said, pointing past the skyscrapers of Century City toward the sparkling ocean.

"I love California on days like this," I said. It was true. British Columbia had the same ocean of course, but the number of days the sky was clear enough to see it were fewer and farther between.

"You from here?"

"Nope. British Columbia, Canada."

"The West Coast, though."

"Same time zone. Wetter weather."

Henry pulled a small, sleek smartphone from his pocket. "Can I get your number?"

Flustered by his question, I dropped the dog's leash twice. "Um, sure. Let me type it in."

Like I hadn't had the same name for nearly thirty years, I misspelled Sabrina, then Lynch, then screwed up the phone number twice. Scared I was going to drop his phone down into a deep crevice on the side of the mountain, I pushed it back toward him after I'd tapped "Done" in the Contacts app.

He looked down, tapped a few keys. Then shoved it back into his own pocket.

"Texted you, so you have my number too. So, I'll see you around?"

"Oh, right. You're going back to the store." He was of course continuing on toward Mulholland, while I had to turn and head back down the hill toward home and work.

"Yep, back to the grind." He said it as if the job weren't his favorite. I'd always assumed that he loved the place. But maybe it was more of a case of service with a smile than true enjoyment. That's how my work on Etsy had been. Opening my own business had brought back my love of jewelry design.

"Me too. Got to get back to work. Awards season and all that."

Henry looked hesitant to go. He knelt and patted Spencer one last time, then stood, his hands shielding his eyes from the sun.

"Again, I'm really sorry about your dog," were my parting words.

Awkwardly, we both turned in opposite directions.

When I got back in cell range, I checked my phone. Nothing. No green or blue bubble announcing an incoming text. The tiny bit of hope I'd cradled in my chest flew away like a delicate butterfly. And like a butterfly, I'd never see it again.

I wanted to kick myself for being so gullible. Henry was just being nice. It happened a lot in L.A. I'd make some stupid Canadian self-deprecating comment. The guy I was talking to felt bad for me, and full of well-meaning sympathy, asked for my number, then never called. Because as much as guys said they didn't always want to date models and actresses, the reality was quite a bit different.

Whatever.

I needed to get back to work. Speaking of actresses. One was wearing my custom creation to the Golden Globes and another dress designer had asked me to complete a complementary statement necklace for the Oscars. The good times had rolled before the Gemma Hart disaster.

If I wanted to fund Kilimanjaro and pay my mortgage, I had to get my mind off eyes as blue as the sky and onto precious and semi-precious stones. These may be my last big commissions for a while. Notoriety had halted the inflow of new work.

Back home, I unhooked Spencer. He loped to the

water dish, sloppily spilling water all over my tiled kitchen floor. Snatching the towel from the oven handle, I bent to wipe the puddle and drips before I tripped, slipped, and banged my head on the stone countertops.

Feeling my head, I figured out that there wasn't any blood from earlier that I missed. I hated that I had to be so careful of every bump, scrape, and bruise. Convinced that I was fine and not on the verge of a hemorrhage, I removed my new, still-stiff trail shoes and stepped toward the living room.

"Ouch," I cried out. Something was under my sock-clad foot. Damned dog had probably left a toy or piece of rawhide near his bowl. Lifting my foot, I spied what was underneath.

What on earth?

It looked like the cameo from before. For the life of me, I couldn't remember having just tossed it on the floor. Hadn't I left it on the counter or the table by the door?

The problem with living alone, or nearly so, was I couldn't blame the movement of objects on anyone other than Spencer. And other than the odd sock or rubber squeak toy, the dog didn't move much around the house.

Batting away the thought of ghosts, I rubbed my fingers against the engraving one more time.

The poem I hadn't thought I'd memorized came unbidden to my mind once again.

> *Love has this jet to which she clings*
> *With ivory and circling locks about*

Bone within silver to cast fear out
Love once found has need of no such thing
Set it free on a pair of dauntless wings

Maybe I should have majored in English and not fine arts. No one made the tabloids after dropping a Shakespeare compendium, although I'd have probably been the first.

Conscious of what I was doing this time, I stuck the cameo in my junk mason jar between three pairs of scissors, needle-nose pliers, countless paper clips, and a corkscrew. I'd take it to my friend and neighbor Mona Love later for her thoughts on it. But first, lunch. All that hiking and heart palpitations from training or Henry or whatever had me starving.

I checked my phone one final time before deciding I needed to put it away. Nope, no message. I was almost one hundred percent sure I'd done my name and number right that last time.

I tried not to let the disappointment get to me. Instead, I focused on making my smoked salmon tartine as close to the one I loved from the Fish Hook restaurant in Victoria. There was always another salmon in the river. I just had to find mine.

Chapter Four

HENRY

HI, my dog died, you wanna date? weren't exactly the words I'd said, but in my mind, they might as well have been. Those had to be the seven worst words in the English language. Maybe not George Carlin bad, but pretty crappy nonetheless.

My clumsy come-on rang like discordant bells in my ears with every step I took across the ridge of the Santa Monica Mountains. Gorgeous views of a sparkling ocean on one side and snow-capped mountains on the other couldn't help me shake the feeling that I'd stuck my hiking boot into my mouth.

How much had I botched that one? I'd wanted to ask Sabrina out for going on six months. I'd seen her on the hiking trail when I'd greeted her with a big smile and said hello in the middle of a hot, dry summer. I had thought we'd shared a bit of a spark. A little fire had flickered in my belly every morning our eyes had met. But like a dumb guy, I'd turned hope into assumption that it was mutual.

Now I wondered if she were just Canadian. Folks from over the border tended to be some of the friendliest people in North America. Now I was the guy who mistook friendly for something more.

In what felt like no time, I was done with the hike at the back door of Canyon Country Mart. Back to work without Sadie. Back to trying to get my parents to expand their beer and wine selection. I tried to breathe away the sense of disquiet gathering in my belly like a hunk of undigested mashed potatoes.

My father was also breathing heavily, as if he'd been the one hiking up the steep incline to Mulholland in the strong California sun.

"The deli delivery is late," he puffed out not one second after I opened the screen, jingling the bells above it. "Can you call Sal to see if they're caught up in traffic or forgot about us again? I'm telling you, Sal's as young as me, but can't seem to remember the time of day." Yep, all of that from my dad five seconds through the door. Was gonna be one of those days.

"I was going to make a phone call," I said, hoping to put off the day's list of tasks for at least a few minutes. I only wanted a little bit of time to bask in the glow of successfully asking Sabrina out. Maybe put together a first-date plan. I was wondering if the beach would be too cold this time of year when my father spoke again, impatience shading his tone.

"You've had more than an hour to make calls. Had to be world's longest hike."

"Seriously," I said. I gave him the look that said he needed to back off.

"Henry. God. I'm sorry. I know that you're broken up about your dog. But you know we can't make sandwiches without roast beef, ham, or cheese."

I fingered the phone in my pocket. I'd only been planning to walk across the center to the one place I could get a good cell signal on this part of Mulholland Drive. I'd only wanted to make sure my text to Sabrina had gone through. Maybe set up a time to go out. In a perfect world, I'd have liked to talk with her a couple more times, had a coffee, maybe put a little bit of distance between Sadie's death and dating, but when Sabrina had announced her plans to travel to far-flung Tanzania, I'd fast-forwarded. Seize the day and all that.

"The phone isn't going to dial itself..." My dad looked at me expectantly.

I shoved the cell deeper into my pocket, took off the hat that was making me too damned hot, and made my way to the small office behind the store's paper goods corner where the landline worked perfectly.

The workday started out with Sabrina at the forefront of my mind, but soon the market took over like it always did. It was one of those days when one disaster came after another. Sal had forgotten our deli delivery, so we had to cancel a sheaf of lunch orders.

The dairy delivered was curdled like cottage cheese.

Somehow the truck driver hadn't noticed the air conditioner had died somewhere between Fresno and Los Angeles, along the hottest miles of freeway in the state. By closing time at eight, all I wanted to do was grab a beer, watch a little mindless television, then go to bed.

I'd pulled off my most comfortable leather boots and was about to prop my feet on the small living room's ottoman while I thought about dinner, when there was a call from down below.

"Honey!" That was my mom.

Legs down, I shuffled over to the small balcony off my living room. I leaned down to see the top of her short, spiked hair. The dark red looked a lot better on her than him, but hers was now doctored by the best in Beverly Hills.

"Just about to eat dinner," I said. Wasn't quite true, but the fact that I needed a break from my parents didn't seem like a nice thing to yell back across the wooded yard we shared.

"Please tell me you haven't cooked anything," my mom called up.

"No, Mom." I sighed, knowing what was coming next. The invitation.

"Great. I've made your favorite, chicken enchilada casserole!"

And there it was, the invitation to dinner. Chicken, cream cheese, canned chilies, and Monterey Jack hadn't been on my favorites list since I'd turned eighteen and had gone to college in New York City. Those first months at NYU had exposed me to a world of food I'd never experienced in Los Angeles. Four years working as a bartender and assistant sommelier had refined my tastes even more.

"I'll be over in a minute," I called down.

Technically, I lived alone. In a nine-hundred-square-foot house. Off Mulholland Drive. A great location by any standard.

In reality, my house was a guesthouse. The main house belonged to my parents not more than one hundred feet away. More than once after moving back from Manhattan, I'd looked for an apartment or a house I could rent. But every time I'd talked about a potential move to my parents, they'd pulled me back in. Jill and Chester Barnhill were more persuasive than the mob. Which was why I was putting my boots back on for a pseudo Mexican cheese casserole.

I walked through the yard, past the open French doors and into the dining room. I went to the cupboard and started pulling out dishes and utensils to set the table the same way I'd done since I'd been old enough to reach the cutlery. The drawer next to it was surprisingly empty.

"Dad, where are the napkins?"

Dad wandered in, tall glass of soda in hand.

"Want wine?" The question was slightly sarcastic. Although, if I'd said yes, my father would have served it with a big smile. A hundred years in customer service had taught Chester that.

"Soda will be fine, thanks. Napkins?"

"Oh, your mom moved them to the kitchen. We don't eat in here too much anymore."

I went through the archway to the kitchen and pulled open one drawer after another until I located the brightly patterned cloth my mother had purchased in Mexico or Arizona or somewhere on one of my parents' Southwest vacations.

"Where's Mom?"

"She'll be down in a minute." My dad took a large gulp of his drink.

The piercing beep of the oven timer pulsed through the room.

"I've got it," I shouted to no one in particular. Bubbling cheese and meat in a deep glass dish greeted me as I opened the oven door. Sliding mitts onto both hands, I lifted the casserole and put it directly on the trivet my mom had placed next to the range.

The click-clack of Mom's shoes sounded on the stairs. She patted my shoulder. "Thanks, honey. Go sit down next to your dad. I'll serve."

Dad was already sitting at the small round table. It had four seats. Two for my parents. The other two had always been for my brother and me. Parties and guests had been outside at the tables or benches around the pool. Our dining room had always been family only.

"Busy day," my dad sighed.

"Yeah, Dad, they're all busy days." I was exhausted with running and keeping up with all the little store details. It was a good thing I wasn't going to have to do it much longer. I was so close to my store that I could almost taste it. Certainly I could visualize it from the gray display racks to the smoked glass temperature-controlled fridges I planned to have along the back wall.

Deli meat, domestic beer, and cigarettes would never be my passion. I regretted that I hadn't even had a moment to look at the importer's new wine list. I wanted to spend at least half a day studying it, see if there were some new French red blends I could add to the store for those who wanted more than beer and cigs. Many of the blends went great with pasta, meats, even the heavy salads our customers preferred.

"I'm thinking about hiring some help," my dad said, leaning forward with an earnest expression. "That's kind of what we wanted to talk to you about."

Relief exploded through my veins. I'd finally gotten through to them, gratified that at least they weren't asking me to take over the store. I could still go on doing the research and preparation for my long-term plans. I felt buoyed by a renewed sense of energy, the earlier tiredness gone.

When I tuned back in to the room, I noticed my parents' eyes on me. I must have been quiet too long. They were looking for a reaction to their news, their long-delayed acquiescence to one of my suggestions. I put a wide smile on my face.

"Great news. I've been trying to convince you to get more than part-time help for years." It was always like this. I shared an idea to make the business money, or make it easier on the two of them. They looked at me like I was a precocious seven-year-old, then said no.

Sometimes, months later, like tonight, they came around. That's how I'd gotten my small but curated wine section, and now apparently a shop clerk. The rest of the time, they made a lot of noise, then did the same thing they'd been doing for the last thirty-plus years.

"Why now?" I couldn't resist asking.

There was a lot of spooning out of food, pouring of drinks, scooting in of chairs. I braced myself once again. Something *else* was coming down the pike and it was probably more than a part-time assistant. They probably wanted my hard-won wine corner for a slushy machine.

"Good casserole," I said to my mom forking my way to the inevitable announcement. The food was good in its own way. Probably would be better with cotija, fresh chiles, and some kind of artisanal salsa. Sparkling red Lambrusco, Spanish Garnacha would be a good accompaniment.

I didn't say a word about my recent consultation with a local chef who was making a huge splash in salsas and hot sauces. I'd learned the hard way. They weren't interested in any of that information.

"We talked to your brother today," Mom said.

Maybe it wasn't the business. My brother, Evan, was a doctor. He'd started working on movie sets, then took his show on the road working in dream vacation destinations. Practicing medicine on resort skiers in Tahoe and island vacationers in the

Caribbean. Perfecting his skills on jet-setting minor royalty.

Hard life. He hadn't worked at the store since he'd left for college.

"Where is Evan?" It was December. My bet was on Aspen or Swiss Alps.

"Bora Bora," Mom enthused. "It's the most beautiful place. Do you want me to get the laptop, so you can Skype with him too? You should see the sand and water. He called from the beach today. The beach, can you believe that? They have internet right by the ocean."

I sorted through what little I knew of tropical islands. "Bora Bora. Is that Tahiti?"

"Yes. I was there way back in seventy-five filming one of those beach movies that were popular then." My mom stood and walked over to the breakfront. After she opened and closed a few doors, a large piece of dark, shiny wood surfaced from one of the bottom cupboards.

"It's a kava bowl," she said. "There were these great woodworkers on the islands. The studio bought me black pearls, of course, but this really reminds me of the islands."

Mom laid the bowl on the table, then disappeared through the French doors. In a few minutes, she was back with a few fragrant magnolia blooms she arranged in the kava. "Not quite those lovely gardenias they had. Chester, do you remember what those are called?"

"Tiara? No, that's one of those crowns Miss America wears. Damn." My father shook his head woefully. "I'd lose at *Jeopardy* today."

I looked between my parents. They were acting weird. Not weird exactly. This was how they were. Mom, doing her flighty former actress thing, reminiscing about the glory days of Hollywood. Dad, indulging her flights of fancy. We all pretended that she wasn't a math genius who kept meticulous books and kept the store running like a well-oiled machine.

"Did you guys want to tell me something?" Mom hadn't done the former actress routine in a long time. Dad was on his second soda. If he had anymore he'd fly away on all those bubbles.

My mom sat back down at a spot different than her usual place. She was never one to eat much, maintaining her figure for any possible career resurgence, however improbable. She drummed her finger against the raffia placemat.

Dad pushed his half-finished plate away, a first.

"We're thinking of visiting Evan. He's going to be there another three months, he said."

Which would, of course, put the burden of minding the store completely on me and this theoretical help. What else was new?

"How long were you thinking of going?" I asked. Not begrudging them a vacation, exactly. Everyone deserved time for rest and relaxation. Los Angeles wasn't France though. They couldn't put up a sign announcing a six-week vacation closure and expect shoppers to understand or come back.

If silence could echo, it would have in my parents'

bungalow. If I'd been uneasy before, I was about to fall into a panic. I braced myself.

"A month, maybe. If your mom likes it, then two."

"Months? Months in the South Pacific?" I tried to put together how I could juggle starting a new business while running the old one. Maybe I could postpone...

"Then you'll be back? When? February?"

My parents looked at each other. They didn't look guilty exactly, but even more uneasy than they had moments ago if that were possible. How heavy was that second shoe going to be? Boot-sized I imagined.

"Not exactly, hon. Your dad and I want to retire. It's December. We're thinking we could finish out the year, then in January, we'll start a new chapter in our lives."

"And the store?"

Mom got a big smile. An outsized smile. An actress's smile. "That's why we called Evan. We wanted to make sure it was okay if we left the store to you."

"You're not dying, Dad? Mom? Is this why you've been at the doctor so much?"

"No, not dying. A little, well, maybe a lot of acid reflux. Leaving it was a bad choice of words. Not leave it to you. Give it to you—now. You do such a good job with it. We thought it would be a great way to protect the Barnhill legacy."

"That's great," I said trying to gin up the enthusiasm a normal person would have. My parents had just offered to give me a fairly lucrative business that I knew I could make even more so. If only deli meat and ice cream were my passion instead of wine and food pairing.

"Maybe you could add that fancy cheese to the sandwiches. Havarti or Brie instead of Muenster or American. I think Sal has some of that on the new order form," my father said in a nod to my ambitions.

As if an order of artisan dairy products or an Italian espresso machine should be enough to satisfy me.

My parents talked at me for another hour about how great it was going to be. How much my future was set. Also, since I was staying in the guesthouse, could I mind their bungalow as well? I wanted to stand up and tell them that twenty-four-hour labor may be called slavery in some quarters. I kept my thoughts to myself, though. I was used to that. It was our family dynamic.

After dinner, they were practically bouncing with enthusiasm over their future travels. As I walked through the yard, I thought I may have heard the words RV and cross-country trip drifting on the breeze. Good for them. They'd shaken the yoke that was Canyon Country Mart. Only *I* wanted to do the same.

But it wasn't mine really. I couldn't sell up because they hadn't signed anything over to me, nor were they planning to. Instead their deal was that I would receive all the income from the store, and later, after they died, my brother and I could sell, I could buy Evan out, or something else. They didn't care, though, about what happened later. It was the idea of selling the store now while they were around that seemed to drive them around the bend.

Back in my own living room, I thought about calling Sabrina. Giving into the pleasure and anticipation of a first date. Instead, I did the responsible thing.

I lifted my laptop from the shelf under the widescreen television. From what I could tell, real estate agents didn't eat or sleep or do anything other than breathe deals. Not ten seconds after I had tapped out an e-mail and hit send, did I have a response.

In a few minutes, I was in my car backing out of the shared driveway and speeding toward La Cienega. The lights were already blazing inside when I parked my car in front of the vacant retail space on Melrose.

"Henry. Good to see you." The agent was dressed like Don Johnson from that *Miami Vice* show that I caught on cable on sleepless jet-lagged nights. From the pastel button-down to the sockless loafers he could have been a dead ringer for Sonny Crockett. I took the proffered hand and shook/half hugged, patting the agent's white-linen-clad back.

"Sorry for the last-minute call, Chris," I said when we broke apart.

Chris lifted his tinted but not quite dark glasses onto his expertly styled dirty-blond hair. "No worries, man. This is an impressive space. It's good you're getting to see it at night. It has exquisite display lighting. The guys before you, the antiques dealers, they did really well here."

Chris opened the door and let me in. The agent had arrived early and done that thing they do—make a space look irresistible. Every halogen spot and flood was on and at maximum brightness. Maybe that's why he wore blue-tinted lenses everywhere.

After walking the perimeter like a cat in new surroundings, I turned to find the agent oh so casually leaning against a large wood desk. It was a brilliant soft sell, not that I needed to be sold. If my parents hadn't dropped their bombshell, I'd probably be signing a lease right then.

"Why did the previous tenants leave?" I asked. Due diligence and all that.

"Divorce," Chris whispered under his breath. "Marriage equality led to divorce equality."

At least they hadn't gone out of business because of zero foot traffic.

"What's going on in the neighborhood?" was my next question. I'd always had a dream about a wine shop in West Hollywood, or Los Feliz, or the upscale stretch of Studio City, but I didn't have granular data on each neighborhood specifically. Agents like Chris who regularly let these spaces had on-the-ground information that could prove invaluable.

"You thinking of doing a wine shop, right?"

"Yeah. I finished my Advanced Sommelier training this past summer."

I'd studied during my off hours and had passed the weeklong exam in Dallas in July, the fourth of five steps on the way to Master Sommelier, a rare achievement I hoped to attain in the next five years.

"And you've done retail before?" Chris asked, not that

experience was a necessity in signing on the dotted line of a net-net-net lease.

"My parents own Canyon Country Mart on—"

"Mulholland. I grew up in Beverly Glen. I used to come there for ice cream all the time in the summer."

As had hundreds of kids over the years. They'd all enjoy their cones on the small porch overlooking the valley then go back home to splash in their pools or play video games with friends. I'd stayed on in the afternoons, more times than not, unpacking boxes and ringing up customers.

"You guys have wine there? I don't remember more than beer, but I haven't been since college," Chris said. Which illustrated half the problem. Well-heeled folks got their wine and microbrews elsewhere. If they needed ice cream in a paper wrapper, or a sandwich in a wax one, Canyon Country Mart was the store to go to. But when they were looking for a hostess gift or ingredients for a night of entertaining, they drove to Beverly Hills, Sherman Oaks, or West Hollywood.

"A bit. Got my parents to add a small selection of quality wines. They've been popular. Want to expand on that with a more appreciative audience."

"Great idea. I can vouch that there is no more appreciative audience than West Hollywood. More double-income, no-kid households than the rest of the county. It's a great complementary business, too.

"You're next to the Pacific Design Center, first off. Second, there are a couple of high-end food places that have opened up. One all-organic Belgian place. Another is a chocolatier. I've got a couple of women who are looking to sell olive oil, balsamic vinegar, and charcuterie a few doors down. Lots of walking in this part of town. Plus, it's the sunny side of the street, but get this. The previous guys installed UV windows and new insulation, so the sun didn't affect the furniture. You could display wine here in a temperature-controlled setting without a crazy high utility bill. I know how important that can be."

Chris's enthusiasm was infectious. The agent was hitting on all the high points that I had covered in the business plan I'd been working on the last couple of years.

"What's the cost, again?" I asked, hoping that the commercial owners hadn't jacked up the price. A yogurt place around the corner was doing amazing business, clogging residential streets with lines wrapping around the block.

I'd only found a parking space when a yogurt-wielding driver had given up her spot. Foot traffic and eyeballs would be gold for the next tenant if they had the right business. I could see tired yogurt hopefuls snagging a bottle of wine for dinner, or coming by after they were done with their confection, looking for something more substantial to take back home with them, since they'd gone through all the trouble to park.

"Only nine dollars a square foot, same as we discussed before. Net-net-net lease. Sure you're familiar with all that."

I walked the eleven-hundred-square-foot space again. It was nice. Pickled-wood floors, highly engineered halogen display lighting. The custom shelves the previous tenants had left would be great for featured wines and shelf talkers. A couple more shelves customized for wine, two or three large fridges for red, white, and to-go selections, and I could be in business.

Well, shelves and inventory. And figuring out how I could run not one, but two retail businesses. If I'd learned anything this morning, keeping the market going was more than a full-time job.

I took the one-sheet Chris had in hand, a copy of the one I already had in my files at home, and reluctantly walked out the door. Chris stepped out with me.

"I'm not one of those agents who pressure you, but this is a popular location that doesn't often come up for rent. Owner's looking for a serious business person to sign a long-term lease. He has a couple of people very interested, so you won't have too much time to make a decision." Yeah, right. So much for low pressure.

The agent ducked back in and started turning off lights. I got into my car and waved to a woman who looked ready for her own yogurt fix.

I wasn't unaware of the irony. My parents were about to have nothing but time. For me, it was running out.

Chapter Five

"WHAT'S THIS?"

Mona Love fingered the cameo on the kitchen counter.

"Don't know. Found it tucked away in a little storage cupboard. It has some wacko poem engraved on the back. I thought maybe I'd go through my files, find the real estate agent who represented the sellers, see if they left a forwarding address."

"Cool, 'cause this thing talks about finding love like it's some kind of cupid's arrow. Can't have that kind of crazy mojo in the air."

"Don't know, I could use some cupid mojo right now," I murmured. Louder, I said, "Some ancient guy probably wrote it for his lady love. Who knows if he never gave it to her or he stored it here or gosh, whatever. How's your work going?"

"Lady love? Did you pull that out of the eighteen

hundreds? Work's crappy. I'm stuck. Lacking inspiration. But I don't want to talk about me. You going to the Oscars?" Mona asked. At least that's what I thought my friend had said. I was too busy obsessing about the phone in my pocket and how it had become the most silent it had ever been.

How was it the thing buzzed incessantly with robocalls and every other person who confused high-end jewelry design with an Etsy shop, but today...today it was curiously silent. Had I somehow broken the thing overnight?

Fingers snapped next to my ear, disturbing the air and my hair.

"Oscars? Earth to Sabrina?"

"Why would I want to go to an awards show in the middle of an afternoon?" To appear on air at night on the East Coast's live feeds, my clients had to be ready for their limos by two or three, the hottest part of the day.

"Let me see. Because you get to wear an amazing dress. You could see your creations up close on a real live actress instead of on TV or in *People Magazine* a month from now. Because it's the freaking Oscars!"

"Maybe I'll try to get a ticket," I said distractedly. Unable to resist the urge, I slipped the smooth glass phone from my jeans pocket and looked at it. "Maybe I'm afraid of another...jewelry malfunction," I said, looking directly at my friend.

"But you're taking precautions, right?"

"Maybe Gemma's London premiere wasn't a good

time to try out something innovative. Something I hadn't really worked out. It's just that she hadn't been in front of the cameras for years and I wanted her to be stunning. Now she's known for sex scandals *and* wardrobe malfunctions. I'll be lucky if I'm invited to the Oscars ever after that."

"So what's the other option, hiding out?"

"Maybe. I kind of understand Gemma a little better now. Who wants to relive their most humiliating moments in front of cameras?"

Which was why I was going to stay home through all of awards season. I found myself looking at my phone again. Hopefully I wouldn't be staring at the phone two months from now. The shiny glass screen was as blank as it had been ten minutes ago, and two hours ago. I shoved it even deeper into my pocket. This Henry-sized distraction was exactly what I didn't need.

"What are you waiting for, a precious-gem delivery?" Mona motioned toward my pocket.

"I don't have hundreds of thousands of dollars' worth of diamonds delivered to my house by armored truck. Talk about calling attention to yourself. I pick them up in the jewelry district and put them in the trunk of the convertible like a normal person."

"Do you really?" Her kohl-black eyebrows shot up in surprise. "I was only kind of joking."

"It's what insurance is for. Most people don't think anything of a tiny six-year-old car."

"Jewelry transport is fascinating, but back to the

phone. You're not that person, you know. The person who I can't talk to or drink coffee with or eat lunch with because you're always looking at your phone. What gives?"

"I'm waiting for a call." My response was purposefully cryptic. Waiting for a boy to call was so 1998.

"From who if not your diamond guy?"

I'd never talked to Mona about guys. Mainly because I didn't date much and Mona didn't date anyone long enough to spark a chat, so there was nothing to talk about.

We were young artists dedicated to building our portfolios and careers, not guys. But maybe Mona could keep me from acting like a stupid intermediate schoolgirl with a crush.

"Have you been to Canyon Country Mart?"

"Sure, who hasn't. Did you order lunch? 'Cause I'm starving. Did you get enough for two?" Took me a moment to realize that Mona assumed I'd made a sandwich or salad order. From what I'd seen, it was the market's primary business.

"No, I didn't order lunch. I like to cook. Made poutine yesterday. Still have a lot left. You want me to heat it up? It's fries with cheese curds and gravy."

"Sabrina, your mind is like a maze and I'm a lost rat. Let's go backward. You're waiting for a call, not about gems, and it has something to do with Canyon Country Mart, but it's not your lunch order, which by the way it's too early for anyway. And poutine? I'd have to lie down for three days to digest that."

"Have you seen the guy who works there?" Because if

Mona had seen Henry, there would be zero questions why I was worrying the home button on my phone.

"Chester? The owner? He's about a million years old and married. Really married. I think he's been married longer than we've been alive. But, yes, I've seen him." Mona's eyebrows had come down and were scrunched over squinting eyes.

At the first "married," I shook my head swiftly because I most definitely didn't play *that* game.

"Not Chester...Henry."

"The guy with the dog. Oh God, him. He's hot. Really hot. Is he single? He can't be single."

"If he's so hot, why haven't you dated him?" I asked, genuinely surprised that Mona had noticed him but not made a play. Mona was the original Sadie Hawkins.

"Really. Seriously. So not my type. I date a lot of guys. A lot of guys. They all have one thing in common, though. And Henry doesn't fit the mold."

I searched my mind, mentally flicking through the boyfriends of Mona's I'd met or seen driving down our dead-end street. They'd been all different colors, heights, weights. Some good-looking. Others, not so much. There wasn't a through line that I could see.

I shook my head. "I don't get it."

"They're bad boys, Sabrina. Tattoos, Harleys, drummers. Your Henry doesn't have a bad or rebellious bone in his body. I could spot his 'good guy' vibes at a thousand paces. Canyon gossip is that he lives with his parents, has since he came home from college. You can rebel in your parents' house at sixteen. Not so much at thirty. He'll probably be carrying his mother's walker one day."

"Oh gosh, his parents. I...uh...don't want to judge, but what magazine would advise dating a guy who lives with his mom? Gah. I'm so glad I talked to you before I made a fool of myself."

"Babe, wait a second. That's totally not fair of me. Sorry I said it. You know how I mouth off. Houses cost a gazillion dollars around here. Lots of people live at home. Doesn't mean he's not a good guy."

"But...mama's boy. Oh God. I can't believe I spent the last twenty-something hours wondering why he didn't call or at least text." A wave of relief washed through me. I'd dodged the dating bullet. I needed to get back to my work anyway. Awards season was only getting closer, ramping up to full speed second by second.

"Is that why you're checking your phone?"

"Was. Going to stop now. I sort of ran into him yesterday at the park," I said, glad that the itch to flick my fingers over the glossy screen was all but gone.

"What happened? What did he say?"

"I asked him about his dog. Oh God. His dog Sadie, who's dead. And then he pet Spencer. Then I said I was going to climb Mount Kilimanjaro, then he said something about going out, maybe."

"Ohh. Sounds like a plan."

"I've checked out the reviews and have finally landed

on a couple of climbing guides. I'm going to decide this week. Maybe toss down a deposit."

"And we're off in the maze again. Let's leave Tanzania and get back to the market at the top of the hill. You're going out with Henry?"

"Even if he probably wasn't a mama's boy, maybe not. I could have sworn he said he'd text me as soon as he could. Twenty-four hours is a long time for soon. Maybe his parents took his phone and he's grounded."

"Ha. Funny. Did you put your number into his phone?" Mona asked.

I nodded. I'd done my part.

"Did he do the same?" Mona prodded. I looked at Spencer, who was nosing against my leg and thighs. A walk would be good. Mind off Henry and back on achieving an earring design that would complement the rose gold pendant I'd made earlier in the week.

"No. I figured he'd text, then I'd have it, but I'm thinking it doesn't matter too much, now that you've given me the lowdown on his life." I was being way too harsh and judgmental, probably, but it was an easy out from doing what I feared—pursuing Henry.

Strains of neighbor sex filled the air.

"Oh God, Allen! Do it to me."

"Ten o'clock," we said in unison and locked eyes.

"Shit. I'm going to get my sneakers. Gimme ten."

"Mona, what sneakers? Hiking during morning sex fest is my thing, not yours. Your thing is heavy metal through noise-canceling headphones."

"I have them. Sneakers, not sex fests. Actually, I have those too, but with the windows closed. Anyway, let me get my running shoes."

"Did you get them at the Doc Marten store?" I asked. All of Mona's shoes had eyelets. Fewer in the summer, more in the winter. I'd never seen so much steel-reinforced toe outside of a British Columbia logging operation.

"Ha, ha. I'll be right back. Let me know if Maribel orgasms before I get back."

"Gross..." Heat crept up my face as I wavered between the belief that Maribel's orgasms were indeed gross or if I was just hard up and jealous.

"I love to make you blush. Such a Canadian. They have to have sex there. Your population growth isn't zero."

"Spencer and I will be outside," I said, my voice full of the prim and proper my native country had imbued me with.

"It's louder that way. Trust me, I know. If they don't sell their house soon, I may have to soundproof my studio."

"Just go. It's walk time." I watched my friend's tie-dyed boots stalk past Allen and Maribel's house and pop into the mid-century house on the other side of the modern wood and glass monstrosity between us.

A few minutes later, Mona was back in orange trail shoes, lug soles and all.

"You've been hiking?" Mona's idea of exercise was lifting her heavy sculptures into a truck before a gallery exhibit.

"I tried dating a guy like your Henry once. We had to

do a daily Runyon Canyon hike with his brown Lab. It was the longest week of my life." Mona shook her head ruefully. "So how does this work?"

"What? Hiking? You put one foot in front of the other. We go up the hill, then turn around and come down. By then, Allen and Maribel will be done and I can get on with the rest of my day. You know, carting gems around and avoiding diamond heists."

"Where does Henry hike?"

"On this trail. The Hastain trail. He probably comes from the store. Franklin Canyon connects there through the Berman trail on that side."

"Then to the Berman trail we go."

"Wait? What?" I was starting to get the brain maze feeling from trying to keep up with Mona. First I discovered my friend and neighbor has hiking shoes and now this.

"We're going on a field trip. I'm dying for a smoothie and maybe lunch too."

I didn't protest when I should have. Instead I went along because mama's boy or not, he was hot. Of course, Spencer was game for anything. He happily tugged at his leash, did his business, and sniffed after other dogs' markings.

Far too quickly, we weren't more than a few feet from the store. I made a mental note to find a buddy early in my Mount Kilimanjaro hike. Strenuous activity was way easier with a friend to chat with. I'd hardly noticed any muscle pain as we ate up the miles together. Mona was especially great with her outrageous stories from the time she'd lived in an artist commune.

"I don't think we should go," I said. I lifted my right hand just above my sunglasses and peered at the store. A few lingering morning patrons were on the porch sipping coffee. The small grassy spot Sadie had called her own was empty.

"You think he's cute. He thinks you're cute. You're both single. Let's do this thing."

"But you said he lives at home, and he didn't call. Maybe he was being nice."

"I'm all about getting to the nitty-gritty. Let's find out. Don't play games. There's no time in life."

Easy for her to say. Mona owned her feminism and sexuality. Every woman should be so comfortable in her own skin. My steps toward the market's front door were mincingly slow.

"What should I say?" I hated myself for sounding like an insecure adolescent.

"You want me to do the talking for you?"

For a second, I considered it. Then I reconsidered. Mona did not have the right social skills for this.

"No, I'll do it. I can do one date. And if he's never cooked his own meal or done his own laundry, if his mom's in that store sitting on a little stool darning his socks, then I'm out."

"It's a plan."

While Mona let herself into the store through the old-fashioned screen door, I looped Spencer's leash around the post Sadie used to occupy. I hoped, mama's boy or not, Henry didn't take it as some affront to his own dog.

I stooped and admired the murals painted on the outside of the store. Huge flowers and retro advertisements flooded the wood and stucco with color. It made the store stand out from the other beige stucco businesses in the little commercial cul-de-sac on the hill crest.

Nerves that should only belong to a teenager shimmied through me. So stupid. It was just a guy, and one who didn't text at that. I'd go in, watch Mona buy a sandwich, and walk all the way back down with my dog and pride intact. Deep breath exhaled, I opened the screen door.

The next breath was a sigh of relief.

No Henry.

No anybody.

"Mona?"

"Back here," my neighbor called from the refrigeration area. "Want a juice or smoothie?"

"Maybe. What are the options?"

Henry's dad came from a back door next to the cold case. According to a blue and yellow label, he was hefting a large plastic-wrapped ball of turkey meat. "That's turkey, avocado, and sprouts, correct?"

"Yep, Chester. Mixing it up a little."

"I agree, gotta keep it fresh. Speaking of, have you met Henry?"

"In passing. If he's here now, I'd love to," Mona said with a little sparkle in her eye that only I noticed. Chester pushed a button on the counter that sounded a buzzer somewhere in the distance. Ten seconds later, Henry stepped into the main part of the store.

"Sabrina, this is a surprise," Henry said.

"Ah, so that's your name." Chester sliced through the tall sandwich with a flourish. "She's Mona's friend. Kind of wanted you to see how Mona here likes her sandwich done. She's an artist and a lunch regular. Today it's turkey and avocado. She always likes her meat sliced thin, extra mayonnaise, no mustard, bean sprouts instead of lettuce and tomato, and always a bagel. Am I right?"

"Perfect." Mona turned to Henry. "Sorry to hear about Sadie. Sabrina said she ran into you yesterday."

Henry turned a shade of pink that clashed with his reddish-brown facial hair. "I didn't text you last night."

"No worries."

"We don't have a signal up here. Then my phone died." He removed the bricked metal, glass, and plastic from his back pocket. "And I still need to plug it in." He stepped around the counter and pulled out a cord with a flourish. He tethered it and tucked it into a nook.

"It's fine. Mona here is a regular, apparently, and she convinced me to add a couple miles to my hike today. Got to get ready for Kilimanjaro."

"Spencer outside?"

"He's in the little patch...hope that's—"

"It's fine. Happy to share the area with dogs." Henry leaned down, then came up from behind the counter with a white ceramic bowl. Blue-glazed paw print designs ringed the top. "Let me..."

He started toward the door and I followed. Spencer, who'd been lazily licking the pole, stood at our presence and wagged his tail wildly.

"He okay with a little water?"

"I'm sure he'd appreciate it." I walked over to the dog. "Right, Spencer?" I sweet-talked while patting my dog on the head and flank.

Henry turned on a spigot and quickly filled the bowl from a coiled hose. He set it in front of my dog, and despite the fact that Spencer had drunk his fill from pit stops along the trail, he lapped it up.

"I'm—"

"So—"

Our words came out in unison, but so were our heads, unfortunately. As we stood, we bumped foreheads. My sunglasses went flying. Henry was able to snag them from midair.

"Nice move."

"It's not my only one." I hoped the little shiver that shimmied up my spine didn't show.

"Not texting when you say you would isn't one of them," I said, and immediately regretted it. Even to me it sounded a little needy and stalkerish.

"I—"

I backed up a couple of steps. "Let's pretend

yesterday didn't happen." I extended my hand. "I've seen you hiking. Sorry to hear about your dog. I'm Sabrina Lynch."

Warily, he extended his own. "Henry Barnhill."

"Nice to meet you. I hear this is your parents' shop."

"Soon-to-be mine. They laid that on me last night." Which was no doubt why I wasn't first on his "to text" list. When we were all fourteen and had someone else paying our bills, a potential date was always the first priority. At our age, other stuff came first.

"Wow. Big news. Great news. Welcome to the world of owning your own business. It's fun making your own rules and hours. Taxes and endless California bureaucracy, not as much."

"Yeah, I've been taking on a bigger and bigger role over the years, I'm already familiar."

"Are your mom and dad retiring? I haven't been in L.A. that long, but they're practically a legend around here."

"They'll be big shoes to fill, that's for sure. You staying for lunch?" Henry asked as the door creaked open. He jogged over and relieved Mona of some of the stuff piled in her hands.

"That pink smoothie is for Sabrina," she said, dropping the rest on one of the six small square tables that lined the narrow porch.

"I'll let you guys..."

"Join us for a few minutes, Henry. If you can spare them," Mona summoned.

"Sure. I'll be right back," he said and disappeared into the store.

"What are you doing?" I hissed, assuming we couldn't be overheard.

"Think of this as a pre-date. If he's crazy, you can definitely lose his number."

"Crap, I'd have done more than jam on this hat and worn ten-year-old sweats if I'd known your plan."

"You wouldn't have come if I'd shared my plan."

Any more discussion was cut off when Henry came back with his own sandwich and water.

"No lunch, Sabrina?"

Why did his deep voice speaking my name send shivers down my spine and make me feel all warm and tingly inside?

"I made...some potatoes. I'll eat later."

Mona made no move to unwrap her sandwich. "It's a little early for lunch. Let's get down to business."

Henry half rose from the chair. "I should—"

"Sit. You're the business."

I ignored the twist in the pit of my belly. Head-on was the best way to come at life. I braced myself for what was coming.

"You asked Sabrina out yesterday. Let's make a date."

"Mona..." I groaned. What was coming was nearly too embarrassing to stomach.

"What? You're going to break your phone by touching it every ten seconds."

The sharp intake of breath was mine. The heat flowing

through my body was on display. Oh God, did Mona have to reveal how much I'd been anticipating his call?

"And honestly, you couldn't find a second to make sure your text went through?"

"His parents told him they're retiring..."

"Wow. Is the store yours now? Congrats. That's a totally acceptable excuse for not calling. All is forgiven. Now, the date. Does Friday work for the both of you?"

"Friday?" I looked at Mona, loving her and hating her in equal measure.

"Yes, it's the last day of the workweek. The word 'Friday' comes from the Old High German word, *frigedag*," Mona intoned.

"Yes. That works for me," I said. Anything to stop Mona from talking. She had a brain like an encyclopedia.

Mona turned to Henry. "And?"

"I'll pick you up at seven thirty," he said to me. "I'll need your address, though."

Like a Jedi, Mona pulled paper and pencil from the pile of stuff in front of her. "Here's Sabrina's address."

"I guess that's not a state secret," Henry said.

"I live two doors down. If Henry here does anything untoward, I'll have eyes on him." She pointed her index and middle finger at her own eyes then at Henry a couple of times for emphasis.

"I'll be on my absolute best behavior," he promised.

Mona looked between us. I was sure Henry's shell-shocked expression was an exact reflection of mine. Guerilla dating had that effect.

"Don't want my mayonnaise to go bad. Food poisoning is a bummer." Mona stood, packed her lunch in her backpack. She handed me the smoothie and poised to leave.

"Okay, well. See you Friday." I scurried to get my hot-pink smoothie and dog and make it to the trailhead.

I waved a quick good-bye to Henry, hoping I hadn't let fear of loneliness trump common sense.

Chapter Six

HENRY

BEFORE I GOT out of my car, I triple-checked my phone. The reservation was for eight o'clock sharp. I glanced at the car clock. Seven fifteen. It would take twenty minutes to drive to West Hollywood, another ten to valet. I tried not to fifteenth-guess my restaurant choice. While I was wondering if my plans had been a good idea, my boot caught on the running board. The sound of tearing fabric shot my already frayed nerves into the stratosphere.

I looked down at my dark blue five-pocket pants that had seemed like the best balance between California casual and careless. Leaning down, I fingered the torn hem. I tucked the tiny frayed part in the top of my boots. I hoped the soft fabric wouldn't be vulnerable to more tearing or I'd look like a Chippendale dancer and not like first date material. I looked over my shoulder wondering if Mona was watching.

I cursed myself. Shouldn't have worn the new chukkas. These boots had sticky soles like new ones always did out of the box before I could scuff them up properly. I should have just worn my favorite pair of boots. The ones that didn't pinch my toes and make me rip my pants. But I'd wanted to make a really good third impression on Sabrina.

So much for that plan.

Resolved to get the rest of this date right, I slammed the driver's side door to work out my frustration. I couldn't remember if I'd ever been on Sabrina's particular dead-end street. I'd explored most of them when I was a kid with more time than supervision, but nothing in this area looked familiar. Nope, I hadn't ever been here, but the wood-sided stucco house she called home was very quaint. The little iron door in the middle of the black gate surrounding the front of the house stood open. Thankful that I didn't have to figure out the little buzzer, I stepped forward through the gate onto the flagstones that dotted her small front yard.

Before I could knock twice on the bright turquoise door, studded with rhinestones spelling out her street number, it opened.

For the second time, I lost my balance, nearly landing on my date. Sabrina had quick reflexes. Her arms came out and caught me before I could catch myself. I stood, brushing the wrinkles from my clothes. My hands fell away and I stopped worrying about how I looked when I caught sight of her.

"You look..."

"Is it too casual, too much? Sorry, I never know how to dress in L.A."

"I was going to say that you look fabulous." She'd have looked good in a potato sack, but I held my tongue on that one. Instead I reassured her that it was all good because it was mouth-wateringly good. "You're dressed just right. Ready?"

"Sure, let me..." She went back in to toss a bone into Spencer's eager jaws, then she locked the door.

I opened the passenger door, then took Sabrina's hand to help her into the SUV. I was looking at her heels, making sure the little spikes didn't snag like mine had when the thud sounded.

"What happened?"

"It was the sound of my head hitting the side of your car. I overcompensated for the heels."

"You going to be okay?" I asked. We were some pair of awkward klutziness, but I didn't mention my earlier fumble. I wanted to be sexy and cool, not a bumbling mess. No one wanted to date a guy who was a dead ringer for a Chevy Chase character. Clumsy was sexy on her, though. I'd be willing to rescue her any day.

"Yeah, it's fine. Let's go," she said, rubbing her head cautiously. "Can't wait to try whatever you have planned."

The drive to the restaurant was brief. We didn't have a chance to talk about anything more than the weather which was fine because it was all the conversation my nerves could handle.

The valet was at Sabrina's door before the car came to a full stop.

"Be careful this time," I said. I didn't want to have to go to the emergency room before dinner. Blood and bandages were not sexy. And I very much wanted this date to make her swoon, but not fall.

"Yeah, I've got this," Sabrina said. The valet took her hand, doing a much better job of helping her from the running board than I had.

"The dining room or the garden, Mr. Barnhill?" the hostess asked as soon as I gave my reservation info.

Sabrina shivered a little in the cold. The hot-pink blouse, even with the tiny jacket over it, didn't look like it was doing much to keep her warm.

"Inside. A corner booth if you have it?" There was no better place to get close. I wanted to be close to her. She looked amazing, silk blouse clinging to what looked to be a lacy bra. Rhinestones circling a delicate neck I'd spent half the day fantasizing about kissing.

The hostess picked up menus and gave a not-so-surreptitious look in our direction. I pleaded with my eyes for the best cozy table.

"How about here?" the hostess asked, gesturing to a secluded round booth, near a blazing fire. I wanted to kiss her too for this perfect table, but I withheld my affection.

"That'll be perfect," I said. I stepped back to allow Sabrina to sit first. I followed her, closing the gap between us so we were sitting more next to each other and less across.

After the hostess left, Sabrina turned to me. Bubble gum-pink gloss blew all thoughts of polite conversation from my brain. I'd planned to wine and dine her, maybe take an after-dinner walk, then... I couldn't remember what I'd planned to come after *then*. Not now, with the gloss of her lips and the heat of her thigh next to mine.

"What's good here?" Sabrina asked, squinting toward the menu. The dim lights that made the booth a date night winner, also made reading damn near impossible.

"They specialize in burgers."

Sabrina's eyebrows rose for the merest flicker of a second before her niceness smoothed it over.

"Everyone loves a good burger in America, right? I haven't done all the famous ones in Los Angeles yet, Tommy's, Fatburger, or that place on Pico..." She snapped her fingers. "The Apple Pan-pie and burgers, right? I did go to In-N-Out once."

"I know how this is going to sound, but it's not just burgers. I met Ted, the sommelier, in Portland a few months ago. He and the chef wanted to turn the iconic Southern California burger joint on its ear. I know I must sound like one of those pretentious articles about fusion restaurants, but I think there are some great wines on the menu. What do you like on your burgers?"

She turned a genuine smile in my direction, then lifted a single shoulder. "I'm game. What are the options?"

We laughed over the hundreds of different combinations because thirty options were probably twenty-five too many. I settled on a twist on the traditional cheeseburger:

cheddar cheese instead of American, caramelized onions in place of fresh and sirloin over chuck.

Sabrina went for it with habañero-jack cheese, hot green chiles and actual chili. Between her burger choice and her plans to hike one of the world's tallest mountains, she had a sense of adventure. I liked that. It stood in sharp contrast to my life, with its set daily routines and predetermined choices.

"Now comes the fun part," I said. Her enthusiasm was infectious.

Her smile's wattage got brighter. "What's that?"

"Finding a perfect wine for these burgers. Since they serve them all by the glass, we can each get something that brings out the food perfectly."

Fist under the chin, she leaned into me. "So what do you recommend?"

I turned to our server, for once not the least bit grateful for the interruption—like I'd have been if my parents or brother had been there. Sabrina and I gave the server our burger orders, then Sabrina turned to me when the server asked what we'd like to drink.

"For her spicy burger, we'll have the Boomtown Syrah from Washington state. For the cheddar, usually a pinot is best." I tapped the menu. "This Carmel Road is a great one from Monterey. We'll take a half carafe of that."

The server took the wine list and left us alone. Gratefully, blissfully alone.

"I hope it was okay that I ordered the wine."

"You're the expert. Can't wait to see what everything tastes like. I have to admit that I know nothing about wine, except I like a good one."

"Have you had any of your local British Columbia wines? I did a tasting while I was in Portland. We compared Washington, British Columbia, and Oregon."

"A few. My mom loves a good wine. She's Québécois. French Canadian, you know, serious about food. Poutine is the world's greatest insult as far as she's concerned. But my dad is more a beer kind of guy."

"You say that like you secretly love poutine."

The megawatt smile was back.

"And a great beer. There's this one sour Belgian beer that I love with it. It's like I've died and gone to heaven when I take that first sip. My cousins take me to this really good dive in Quebec while my mom and aunt stay home and gossip in French."

I'd dated women from all different walks of life, but never one who wasn't one hundred percent American born and bred. I never knew I could find Canadian so exotic and sexy. Sabrina was full of surprises. I couldn't wait to unwrap more.

Our wine and burgers came quickly, along with water and a sheaf of napkins. At least there was an upside to fast food. It limited the awkward time between ordering and eating. At least I hoped it wasn't awkward, but the way Sabrina was moving her hands around, I thought maybe it was.

"Laying hands on it?" I joked. I racked my brain. She wasn't a vegetarian. She'd said she ate quiche with bacon. I'd never forget that—one of the first facts I'd learned about her. Though there were people who ate pork, but not beef, mostly it was the other way around.

"It's big," she said. My thoughts interrupted, I looked into her big brown eyes. I could get lost in those eyes. Warmth and sincerity emanated from her. I looked at her moving hands again.

"Maybe not so much big as tall. I can't figure out how I'm supposed to pick it up and not end up with the green chiles or chili all over my shirt. Food on your face is cute when you're one, not so much at twenty-nine."

"My mom would use a knife and fork," I said. My mother, who'd been famous in her youth, had mastered the art of eating in public without spilling a drop.

"Would she? Well, that's nice. Are you close?"

Sabrina laid her palms flat on the booth cushion and lifted herself up a couple of inches. In seconds, she'd moved a little bit away on the bench. She made the move like she needed elbow room for burger eating, but that sentiment didn't ring quite true.

"Um, yeah. I work with her every day and I live in her guesthouse. So yeah, we're close," I explained.

"I think this will be easier without my blazer." Sabrina edged farther away as she removed the black jacket.

"That's a nice necklace," I said. The jewelry, which my mother would have called a statement piece, gleamed in the dim lighting.

"I designed it."

"You?"

"I make and design jewelry."

"Like metalsmithing?"

"More or less. I create unique pieces, then put them together in my shop."

"Sounds interesting."

"It's actually a dream come true. This one is for Kimberly Welch. She won an Emmy last fall. Now that she's up for a Golden Globe, she wanted something with a little more sparkle. Trying it out to make sure it's comfortable for more than a few minutes. Celebrities don't like to be poked in the neck."

"How many rhinestones are in that? It certainly does sparkle." My guess would have been close to a hundred, large and small.

"Oh, they're not paste. They're diamonds."

"Seriously? That has to be what, quarter of a million dollars of diamonds?" I was thinking something like that required an around-the-clock body guard.

"More like a half million."

And I'd thought a twenty-dollar burger was rich. "Not that I'm any judge, but I think she'd be crazy not to like it."

She picked up the burger, put it down again. Sighed. The megawatt smile was gone. "After the disaster earlier this month, I'm hoping to redeem my reputation."

"What happened?"

Sabrina fingered the stones, her face contemplative, when one broke free, then another, then another.

"Oh God, no...what am I doing wrong?" she cried before she dove under the table in search of the missing stones.

I followed her because even a fraction of half a million was probably tens of thousands no one could afford to lose. Every time she picked up one diamond, another popped loose. It was like trying to stop a glittering tsunami.

"Here." I gestured with my hand. "Give me the necklace. I'll put it on the table."

Her hands went around the back of her neck and unclasped the heavy piece. She gathered it in her palms and I took the heavy-set stones and laid them on a section of booth. Then I dove under and gathered all the stones I could find.

"Everything okay?" The server's voice floated down to us.

We both jerked up, bumping our heads against the underside of the table. Glasses and utensils rattled. Carefully, I eased my head up. "Everything is fine. My date dropped something."

"Alrighty then. Enjoy."

Sabrina popped back up, three jewels in hand.

"You got them all?"

She lifted the necklace onto the table and spread it out. She matched the diamonds to the empty spaces and sighed in relief. "All there. Can you unzip my purse?"

I followed her direction and opened the leather satchel. Slowly, she poured the necklace in.

"I can't believe... You know what? Let's get back to the burgers before they get cold." Gamely, she took a big bite, wiping away the green sauce that squirted on her chin with the back of her hand.

That single move made me smile from the inside out. She was a real woman with real flaws, and I liked her all the more for them.

"Have you tried the wine?"

"No. But you said this will go with burgers. Better than beer, huh? Okay, here goes."

She took a large sip, but her face was not the picture of sublimity or pleasure. Gently setting the glass on the table, she smiled big.

"Maybe not my thing, this Shiraz did you call it?"

"Syrah, Shiraz. More or less the same grape. Syrah is more a French-style wine; Shiraz is Australian, a bigger, bolder flavor. Washington grapes are somewhere in between."

"Are you going to do a big wine display in the store?"

"My parents' market?" I could feel the joy seep from my body, my face muscles screwing up in a frown.

"Soon-to-be yours, right?" she asked, fist under her chin again. She wasn't eating her burger or drinking her wine. This date was like a seismograph with its ups and downs. Not at all like I'd pictured. I held in my sigh of resignation.

"In a few weeks, yes, I suppose."

"You don't sound happy."

"One of the reasons I didn't call you that day I said I would was because I had an appointment with my agent to see a commercial space in West Hollywood."

I laid my hand on the table. Tentatively, she covered it with hers. Not the wine or necklace mattered much to me at that point. Our eyes met. Heat sizzled between us.

"That sounds cool," she said. Her voice was a lot calmer than the pulse that was jumping in my neck. "Are you going to run two shops?"

"Can't see how I can do that, so I'll work at the market."

"Well, it's great either way." Her voice was upbeat, positive. I wished I could share her feelings about the market. That I wasn't as enthusiastic about it as I was about finally getting to go on a date with her. I'd had to ditch the fantasy of my own store, and maybe Sabrina as well. I wanted to kick myself for taking so long to finally ask her out. Maybe it would have been better before she was too preoccupied with work and me with the store. I sucked in a breath, ready to make the best of it.

"So, your wine?" I asked when she took back her hand and took another bite of her food.

"Maybe I'm more of a beer girl. No big deal."

"Can I have a sip?" I asked.

"Knock yourself out," she said before I lifted her glass to my lips.

The tart, acidic taste hit the back of my throat like a slap in the face. My cough was automatic, though I tried to cover up the spasmodic reaction.

"It's vinegar!" I plunked the glass down with a thud.

"They poured vinegar?"

"No, the wine went off. Poor storage, probably. Bad temperature, cork wasn't kept damp. Those are the main reasons. I'm so sorry that you got that."

"At least that wasn't good wine. Tasted more like kombucha." There was relief in her laugh.

"Gimme a second," I said. I pulled my phone from my pocket and tapped out a text to my fellow sommelier. Not five minutes later, Ted came over to the table, bringing cold with his coat.

"This is Sabrina Lynch. Sabrina, Ted Russell."

"Vinegar? Seriously? I had to come across the street for this," Ted huffed.

"Across the street?" Sabrina chimed in, eyeing his coat.

"The guys who own this place own the French bistro across the street. One of the owners loves burgers, so when the space opened up, he went for it. Turns out great wine and burgers is a successful concept. I think it's a higher table take than La Pomme Prend. I can't tell you the number of bistros that have died in L.A."

"What happened with the Syrah?" I probed. I'd really wanted to make a good impression, and this had not started well at all. Ted was going to be my savior.

"Gimme a second." He came back with glass in hand and poured a bit from the carafe, took a sip, and made a sourpuss face. "Damn. Let me bring you something else. I'll have them take all this away."

Not seconds later, two busboys cleared the table of the

wine and burgers. What followed were plates of baby greens and tiny mussels, miniature crab cakes, and shrimp in sauce.

Sabrina, either hungrier or more enthusiastic than she'd been about burgers, only hesitated a moment before picking up a delicate-looking triangle of pastry and sinking her teeth into it.

"Mmmm. So good."

Ted came around the corner with a flourish. On a large tray, he had six carafes half filled with white, red, and rosé wines. He made a show of pouring tastes and talking about pairings. A sip here and a nibble there, and Sabrina looked like a woman who was being supremely satisfied. I'd wanted to be the one to put that look on her face with good food, wine, or myself.

"These are really good. You should try one," she said, her lips turned up in a smile.

"I'm sorry about the burgers and vinegar wine."

"Aw, Henry. Don't worry about it. Everything is great." She took a seafood fork from her napkin and pulled a mussel from its shell. She extended the utensil to my lips. "Have a try."

I opened and closed my lips around the fork and mollusk. The burst of garlic, shallots, and parsley was a great marriage of flavors.

"So what's good with this?"

"A dry Alsatian viognier." I picked through the carafes on the table. "This one." I poured an ounce in her white wine glass. She took a delicate sip. Then added a mussel and took a heartier taste.

"This is so good. Damn. If this is what you want to do, you have to do it. This is better than sex."

Immediately, Sabrina's open palm covered her nose and mouth in embarrassment. "I can't believe I said that."

"I can't believe it's true."

Her other hand joined the first, not doing a great job of hiding the red stain creeping up her face. She peeked between her fingers, then covered her face again.

"Great sex is not something to be embarrassed about." I hoped to God that sex with her would be a thousand times better than French bistro food.

"I don't even know what to say after that," she said after pulling her hands from her face.

"I say, let's finish this great dinner."

And we did just that. I didn't mention sex again, though once the thought was implanted in my mind, I could think of little else. Suddenly food and wine pairing didn't seem like the most important thing in the world. I wondered how I'd let that cloud my vision.

"Thanks so much for this," Sabrina said after she'd taken a couple of bites of her pot de chocolat.

"Do you like the dessert?"

"It's great. I'm full. Everything was so good. You really know your stuff."

I resisted the urge to preen under her gaze.

"Glad you enjoyed it." I scooted closer to her, the way we'd started the night before jewelry explosions, and took one of her hands in mine. "I had a good time tonight. I'd love to do it again."

The server chose just that moment to come over to our table. Timing was not the waitress's strong suit, it appeared. "Dinner's on the house, courtesy of Ted."

"Thanks," Sabrina and I said.

The mood I'd been trying to build in that moment, trying to build all night, was shot...again. I lifted slightly and removed my wallet from my back pocket. I pulled out two fifties and placed them under a carafe.

"Nice tip."

"The waitstaff and busser shouldn't be penalized."

"Cool." Sabrina shifted away again. "Ready?"

No, I wasn't ready for the night to end. Not really. But I couldn't think of anything else I could do to prolong the inevitable. We were a good twelve miles from a romantic walk on the beach.

After she stood, I followed suit. Then I lifted her jacket by its shoulders and helped her shrug into it. Keeping a hand on her shoulder, I stayed close as I steered us through the maze of tables toward the exit and valet stand.

The ride home was as quick as the one there. In less than ten minutes, I was in front of her single garage door and I'd lost half my age. It was as if I were a teenager all over again. That nervousness that I'd felt on my first car date at sixteen was no different than how I felt now, the churning stomach, lightheaded, and nearly faint with the urge to kiss her.

I'd worried so much about how clean my car was, what

I'd wear, the wine at the restaurant, that I'd put this last part out of my mind. After I pressed the button to turn off the ignition, what came after was the only thing on my mind.

Remembering my manners, I opened my door, stepped down from the car, and came around to her side. The running board was still a challenge, and she tripped, again, falling right into my arms. I set her upright, but Sabrina remained only a few inches away. Her lips, gloss mostly gone, were parted. Her eyes met mine with what I hoped was anticipation.

"Can I kiss you?" I heard myself asking. God, I sounded like such a wuss. Didn't women like guys who took charge, went for it, damned the consequences? Instead, I sounded like a college consent brochure.

"I'd like that," she answered. What followed were the longest and most awkward milliseconds I could ever remember. Then she spoke again. "I'd really like that, Henry Barnhill."

Her use of my name compelled me forward. Her tongue came out, licking her bottom lip in anticipation. I didn't need any further invitation. I cupped her shoulders and placed my lips on hers. After the first moment of hesitation, she slanted her head and melted into me.

Pulling back, I changed the angle that joined our mouths and she opened for me. I couldn't help the groan that escaped me when she inched ever closer, her thin silk top doing everything to heighten the friction between the tips of her breasts and my shirt.

Sabrina drew back. For a long moment, I was worried that I'd gone too far.

"Do you want to come in?" she asked.

My horny self had the world's shortest debate with my sensible self.

"Yes, I would."

Chapter Seven

SABRINA

STANDING in the doorway between the dining room on my right and the living room on my left was a living, breathing, man. As Henry bowed slightly to pet the very excited ridgeback spinning around the basalt tile entryway, I cast my eyes about as if there were a script, or a director, or God would appear out of thin air and tell me what to do next.

I opened my mouth. Then I snapped it shut as quickly as I could. I'd been about to do what my mother always did when guests came over: offer wine. Somehow, the candy-pink-colored white zinfandel I knew to be inside my refrigerator door didn't seem like a good thing to offer to a sommelier.

"Please have a seat." I pointed to the plum-colored button tufted sofa. Then I nudged Spencer toward the yellow wingback chair he'd long ago claimed. The dog didn't have to be invited twice. Happily, he jumped on the seat, did his two or three usual turns, then curled up nose to tail with a contented sigh.

Henry did that thing men did, pulling up his trousers a couple of inches on his thighs. I looked down toward his boots. He had some weird tear in his pants. It looked like the kind that had started small, then crept up his leg. If he didn't do something it would be at male-stripper level soon. Best not to mention that to him, though. The thought of his pants magically melting away was kind of appealing.

I watched Henry sink back into the couch. It had taken an act of Congress to get the extra-deep velvet sofa into my house, but I loved the twin-bed-size cushions. It was my happy place to think, watch TV, and hang out with Spencer. And now Henry was there. By the looks of it, it was going to take a presidential executive order to get him out of the cushions and into make-out position. I shook my head, trying to free it of the stupid American government analogies. Civics was not as interesting as sex.

Sex, or the thought of the prelude to it, was making me giddy and heedless. Got me thinking that Henry was the kind of guy who'd make it different—this time. Who wouldn't care that I was less than perfect. Who would give me satisfaction so I didn't have to do it vicariously by neighbor.

Living next door to the Grissoms was a daily exercise in torment and frustration about what I was missing. Every screaming orgasm I heard through my studio window reminded me I wasn't having one that day, or the day before, or any day after.

Okay, maybe not none, I did know where the closest adult toy store was, and had patronized it more than a couple of times. But not one that involved another person.

Now I had my very own person, and I had no idea what to do with him. No idea how to navigate the thorny issue of the long scar that bisected my breastbone. Something I most often hid with high-necked blouses and camisoles.

"You want some wine?" The stupid request had come out of my mouth even after I'd told my brain to keep it in. But I'd wanted something to say that didn't start with reasons why I was self-conscious about my body. "Sorry. That was stupid. I only have cheap wine here."

"Wine doesn't have to be expensive to be good." He didn't sound so much convinced as polite. I wouldn't be pouring the pink wine.

"Right. Gotcha. Um, what happened to your pants?" He should know he had the melt-away pants.

Henry looked chagrinned. "Tore it stepping down from the SUV before I knocked on your door."

I had to smile a big smile. Either this date had been a huge freaking disaster or was the best date ever. I was leaning toward best ever. It was awkward good, not awkward bad.

"That car is a menace."

"I know." His headshake was rueful. "It's new. Got it to make it easier to haul around wines. It's got a big temperature-controlled cabin."

"And evil running boards." Our shared laugh did little

to break the tension. I walked from the fireplace to the wingback, to the side table, where I stilled long enough to finger the creepy cameo then drop it back into my random key and paperclip jar. I was starting to think the thing had some kind of special powers. A poem about love appears one morning, and a hot guy is in my living room a few days later. Either special powers or one hell of a coincidence.

"You're pacing," Henry said, his voice low and rough. "I don't have to stay if I make you uncomfortable."

"Don't leave," I said, my voice too loud for the moment. I waved my hands in front of my face, trying to hide all the feelings I didn't want on display. "I'm behaving like I'm in grade nine." I came to a stop, my shins brushing against the velvet. "Can we try the kissing thing again?" Because more than wine or food or dessert, I wanted to try the kissing thing with Henry again.

"You don't have to ask twice."

Henry grabbed my hand and pulled me down to the couch. It wasn't anything like a good rom com. I didn't fall into him daintily. Instead, my palm went to his chest to keep the majority of my weight off of him and not add crushing injury and ambulance ride to our night of wins.

My worry disappeared the minute I turned off the inner critic in my head. Henry's muscles were firm and hard. They were very nice—all his hard parts.

Whether I pushed him or he fell back himself, I didn't know. In seconds, we were all over each other. I wasn't the only person ready to act on our attraction, thank heavens. My eyes met his and my movements slowed.

The intensity of his stare made me as tingly as his touch. Blinking, I looked at his hair. Slowly, I sifted my hands through the short strands, glad that it wasn't full of wax or mousse or any kind of stuff. With my thumb, I rubbed first his top lip, then his full lower lip, the springy hair there tickling the pad of my finger.

"I've never kissed someone with facial hair."

"And..."

"The verdict is..." I leaned down and placed my lips on his. So good. Firm, soft, and full of intention, he slanted his lips, changed the angle of the kiss. Time disappeared as we turned this way, then that, tongues dueling. Breathing heavily, I leaned back, but only a hairsbreadth apart.

My focus was on the lips that were making me tingly, on his earlobe that attracted my teeth, on the cords of his neck that vibrated under my tongue.

Twitchy. Hot. Jittery with desire. I was all of those things. All at once.

With a single shove, I had the scratchy soft sweater and the thin shirt under it up and away from the hot plane of his belly. The front of him looked as good as it had felt pressed against me.

Tiny whorls of red-brown hair sifted through my fingers. The combination of that and the scruff on his face tickled at different spots on my body, making me aware of at least a hundred different points of contact between us.

One minute I was in control, on top, deciding the slant of our lips, the thrust of our tongues, the amount of clothes that were on or off, and in the next he'd rolled me so that he was on top.

I tried to swallow my gasp, my hesitation, when his hand slipped under the back of my blouse.

"Is this okay, what we're doing?" Henry asked. His eyes were both tender and blazing hot with desire.

Yes, it was most certainly okay, I wanted to shout. But for another entirely different reason that made zero sense, it wasn't okay.

Instead of answering, I lifted his sweater the rest of the way off and then pulled him down so our lips met again. Wasting no time, I slipped my tongue inside his mouth. The sweet honeyed taste there was like manna from heaven.

I'd missed this part of life so much. But I was so out of practice, so unused to being out among the living, that it was like I was drugged or drunk. The sips of dozens of different wines had probably made me tipsier than my usual single glass of whatever was on sale at Trader Joe's.

In a move I hoped wasn't obvious, I prodded Henry onto his back. Pulling back, I smoothed my hand through his hair, then traced the outline of his short beard.

"I can't believe this is your real hair color," I whispered. "Most women I know would kill to have hair the color of oak leaves in autumn."

"It's hair that made my mom famous."

My move away from him was so abrupt, a couple of the sofa pillows scattered on the floor.

Henry's hands covered his eyes as if in prayer.

"I can't believe I just said that."

"So, moms are not sexy," I said. "Not that moms themselves can't be sexy. They have to be to become moms. But your mom, not so much right now."

"Yeah, I know." He sat up halfway, plumping a pillow behind the small of his back.

Moving to the far corner of the couch opposite, I mimicked his actions, pillowing my back to make it more comfortable. Before I spoke, I tried to convince myself that it was his mom that broke the mood. That my fear of him seeing me naked, finding out the truth that scared most guys away, wasn't at all an issue.

"Do you know what the gossip is about you?" I asked. Even at this far end, five feet away, his scent, cologne, soap, and that indefinable scent of man intoxicated me, drawing me to him like a moth to a flame.

"Gossip?" Henry's brow furrowed. "About me?"

"Henry, you're a hot, single guy who works in a very public place. I imagine lots of people talk about you."

His brow wrinkled even more, as if he couldn't imagine being the subject of rumors, much less the subject of sexy dreams. He really had no idea.

"What do they say?"

"That...well...you live with your parents. Not like you're in the basement playing Dungeons and Dragons or anything, but that you're close to them. Don't go out much."

I stopped because nothing I was saying was making it

any better. If anything, much worse. "I'm not trying to make you feel bad. I'm just kind of wondering..."

Why he wasn't already taken. Hot, single guys were rarer than rainstorms in Los Angeles. If he was available or if he was unnaturally tied to his parents in some way that made dating impossible. All that was getting ahead of myself though, so I just stopped talking.

He hunched over his thighs. Heat radiated from him. I wanted more of that heat, but the wise part of me knew that answers were better now than later, when you were in too deep to care that they were crazily flawed.

"I live in a guesthouse," he explained. His sigh was a huff of air. "It's an apartment across the property."

"As a single woman of a certain age, there are men who get ticked off the list of eligible," I started, then damned my running mouth. But from the intense way he was staring at me, I thought I ought to continue my uncharitable explanation of the rules single women followed. "Those who are not straight, and maybe not out; those who care more about money than people—you know, studio heads, agents, plastic surgeons and the like. Those who care more about cars than people—the Ferrari drivers speeding down Sunset on Sunday...and..."

"Let me guess. Those who live with their moms. Who you all assume can't do their own laundry, cook their own dinner, or think for themselves."

"I didn't say that." I checked my short-term memory. No, I was sure I hadn't voiced those thoughts out loud.

"You didn't have to."

"I really like you. I just need to know, I guess, if you fit in any of the above categories. I don't want to invest in something that can't go anywhere." And now I'd revealed way too much. What if he was in it only for a one-night or three-night stand? Now he probably thought I had us walking down the aisle. If he was stuck in his basement, I looked like a bunny boiler.

Henry sat up and scooted over to my side, the soft velvet making for an easy glide.

"I really like you, Sabrina." He tipped my chin so I had to meet his eyes. "I don't love that new car. After tonight, I may pry the running boards off that thing, resale value be damned."

I had to laugh at that. At least it didn't seem like he took himself too seriously.

"I'm no movie mogul. I didn't make deals for breakfast or lunch today. And you know where I had dinner. With you, because that's where I've wanted to be since I asked you out. The mention of my mother was so stupid. I love her, don't get me wrong. But other than the occasional casserole she forces on me, she doesn't cook my meals.

"I know how to use the washer. I know what a spin cycle is. If I weren't saving up for inventory for my new shop, I'd probably have one of those new apartments in Studio City near Whitsett or Tujunga. I also know that I want to go back to kissing you, undressing you, and making you feel as good as you're making me feel."

He didn't need to ask twice. His mouth was close

enough that the words "feel good" ruffled my hair, blew along my neck, made me feel amazing.

"Lift your arms," I commanded. He did as I said and I lifted his tank over his head. If he didn't know his hair was amazing, Henry probably wasn't aware that his chest and arms were the stuff of fantasies. Not that gym workouts were a bad thing, but lifting heavy boxes of wine and hiking had done his body good. "You look so strong," I whispered, before covering one of his nipples with my lips and tongue.

I thought he'd nearly sail off the couch, his body twitched so hard.

"Ooh, you're wired."

"What?"

"It's what they call it when a guy has sensitive nipples." I didn't let him think on that too long. I moved to the other and his response was more muted, but still electric. Kissing my way back up his neck, I took my time getting back to his lips. More deliberate this time, I did whatever I could to stoke him, make him react. When my hand strayed to his buckle and then down to his zipper, the hard bulge let me know I'd been very, very successful.

For long moments, I was only half in the room. The part of my brain not occupied by his hard body and firm lips was working out whether or not I should say something or just casually remove my blouse...or...or...

Indecision pushed me into moving as if on autopilot, and before I could think straight, I was doing what I always did, even though I'd promised myself I'd stop.

I rubbed my lips on his until Henry's eyes glazed over and he looked as if he couldn't think straight. Then I slipped my mouth to his belly button while undoing his buckle and unzipping his zipper. One of my hands focused on massaging his chest while the other pulled his very stiff cock from his underwear.

"You don't... We should..." His protest would be futile, if I had my way.

When my mouth closed on him, all the woulda, coulda, shouldas melted away like ice cream in a blazing-hot Santa Ana wind. I licked and sucked him like he was the best lollipop ever, until he lost all his words. Then I knelt over him, taking him deep in my throat. My other hand left his chest and cupped his balls. Once I got the rhythm right, it wasn't long before he jerked once, twice, then I backed off a bit and pumped his flesh a third time until he came in my mouth. I didn't let go until I'd milked the last from him.

"Ah, Jesus, Sabrina, I didn't... You don't..." The rest of what he was going to say was lost amid a series of grunts and groans that let me know he'd lost the ability to articulate any more words in the English language.

I used the back of my hand to wipe away anything left on my mouth.

Then I remembered my agreement with myself not to do what I'd just done.

Despite all the promises I'd made to myself, I was right back in the same stupid predicament. No doubt Henry thought I was an entirely different kind of girl.

Mortification. That's what stained my cheeks. What in the hell had possessed me to become "that" girl? That girl who was so bold that I blew a guy on the first date. That girl who pretended that a guy's pleasure was my own. That girl I'd promised myself I wouldn't be once I left the great north and came down to Los Angeles. The change of scenery, of my house, of my city, of my country, hadn't really changed much at all.

Henry put himself back together as best he could. His silence felt interminable. I watched the expressions flit across his face. Watched him battle between what he thought was right and what he should say.

"I think we should call it a night," I said, preempting the gentle letdown he was inevitably working through in his mind. Disappointment flashed through me as relief smoothed out the worry lines on his face. "I've got to figure out what's making my jewelry disintegrate all over the place, and you gotta get back to wine hauling in your temperature-controlled cabin and the Canyon Country store."

"Sabrina—" His hand reached out. I moved away as quickly as the lizards that skittered up my stucco retaining wall.

"Thanks for dinner. It was great...the idea of burgers and the tasting menu your friend did. I've learned so much about wine. Who knew that there were so many different wines that could go with so many different foods? Freakin' amazing. It's kind of like you have a super-power. It surely melted my panties. Speaking of which, I need to get upstairs, hop in the shower, get Spencer out one last time."

During my diarrhea of the mouth, I'd helped him get on his shirt and sweater, rescue his wallet from the couch pillows, and herded him toward the door. I was doing a better job than the border collie my parents had once had.

"I want to take you out again, make it up—"

"Right. So let's do that soon. Text me or whatever. It's late, so...good night, Henry," I said as I hustled him to the patio and through the iron fence. I never locked the coded gate, but tonight I did, using the tiny LED light to punch in the code and shut the world out.

With brisk efficiency, I crossed the flagstones and closed my turquoise door. As soon as I knew I was alone I leaned my back against the door, sliding down inch by inch until my butt hit the cold, dark gray basalt at my entryway.

It was never going to change. One congenital defect had broken the rest of me. I wasn't ready to date. I definitely wasn't ready for Henry. Wasn't ready for life, prime time, the big leagues or whatever you wanted to call it. He'd taken me to dinner and I'd repaid his kindness with trying to be nice.

I'd taken nice one step too far.

♥

I HATED the suspense of waiting for bad news. It was in the too-quiet phone. It was in my empty e-mail box. It was in my blank text message screen.

Whether it was doctors telling me it was surgery or a limited life, or the boyfriend who said that a sick girlfriend was too much to handle, I wanted to get it over with now. If Henry thought I was cracked, I wanted to hear him say it. How I'd ruined his perfect date by not taking a bite of the burger, swilling vinegar, acting like a whackadoodle girl who didn't have the sense the provincial school system gave me.

The bleat of my phone nearly sent the pile of diamonds on my worktable scattering to the far corners of my studio. For the last week, I'd been holed up in my place, trying to work out the issues of what was making my jewelry come apart and what made a nice girl act like I didn't have a lick of sense.

In the decade since I'd finished my training, disinte-grating jewelry had never been a problem. I certainly wished it had been in the beginning when it didn't matter, and not now when everything was on the line.

The phone did that mechanical noise thing again, and I dropped my tools, my concentration shattered once and for all.

With equal parts hope and dread, I snatched the phone from the edge of my worktable.

"Mom," I said after eyeing the caller ID with equal parts relief and melancholy. All was silent from Henry, not that I should expect any different. Exhaling disappoint-ment, I said, "I wasn't expecting to hear from you."

"Because you'd told your brother to keep a secret?

Sebastien hasn't been able to keep anything to himself since he was in diapers."

I sucked in a breath, the faint clicking I rarely heard louder with her increasing panic. I wouldn't have told my sieve of a brother a damned thing if he hadn't been in the room with my vault of a sister, Jasmin, and overheard the screaming into the phone.

"I'll be fine, Mom." I stuck a whole bunch of courage and belief and faith into the words. Hoping beyond hope it would block my mother from asking questions.

The hope had been in vain.

"Are you kidding me? You'll be fine. The doctors said mildly rigorous exercise was fine. Traveling to places of higher elevation was fine if you were monitored. But doing both, the exercise and the high elevation, on the side of a mountain, in Africa of all places. I think you have a death wish, Sabrina."

"I'm not suicidal, Mom," I interjected, though I might as well haven't spoken at all because my mother was far from finished with her tirade.

"You haven't been the same since your surgery. Sometimes I think they cracked open your chest and replaced your heart with another girl's. A girl who wanted to break her own parents' hearts. It isn't enough that you've moved two thousand kilometers from where we can keep an eye on you. Now you want to go fifteen thousand kilometers to the middle of nowhere to risk the nine years of good health you've been lucky enough to have."

"I had the surgery to live, not to live like I'm going to die."

I pulled the phone away from my ear so I couldn't hear my mother cry. It was the sound of heartbreak that went straight to mine. The distance from the phone didn't mute the sound coming from Canada. My mother hiccupped then descended into various curses in French. It's why I was able to teach all the kids the bad words in the first day of grade-eight French.

My mother swearing was a rare event and meant that she was in distress. I wanted to hang up. My mother stressed and crying was enough to freak me the fuck out. Had been since I was little and my family had moved from Quebec to British Columbia.

"Have you seen a doctor to discuss this whacky plan of yours?" My mother was nothing if not persistent. As quickly as she was wound up, she unwound. Hysteria was quickly replaced by common sense.

"Not yet."

"Please promise me you won't go off half-cocked without considering all of the consequences."

"Of course not. I've been doing my research. There's a sports medicine clinic in Beverly Hills."

"Does this elite, frou-frou sports medicine team include a cardiologist?"

"Yes," I said. "Of course." I had no idea if it was true. But the likelihood that my mom would consult Google was little to none. "Either way, I'll loop Dr. Ives in. I've just had my yearly in November and he said I was doing well with my level of activity. You know I hike with Spencer every day."

"Hiking a few hundred meters up a hill is not the same as one of the world's tallest mountains. People die hiking Mount Hood, and that's got to be short in comparison."

Changing the subject, I said, "Kimberly Welch is going to wear one of my designs for the Golden Globe awards in a few weeks."

"Who?"

Despite all my protests, my mother had taken to British Columbia as if she were the original pioneer woman during the western expansion. Which included making food from scratch and growing vegetables on our land. All that left little time for current American entertainment.

"She's really famous. I'm hoping that this will launch me to the next level."

"Honey, you're very talented. You don't need anyone to launch you anywhere. Is that what this is about, the thing with that British actress?"

"Wasn't my finest moment."

"It could have happened to anyone."

"I don't think it's ever happened to anyone but me."

"But you don't have to hike a mountain in Africa to prove that you're a good designer."

"That's not it, Mom."

A far-off sound beeped, probably the kitchen timer. "The bread is done with its second rise. Gotta get it in the oven in time for dinner."

"Je t'aime, Maman."

Chapter Eight

SMOOTH TRANSITION WERE NOT the words I would have used to describe my takeover of Canyon Country Mart.

There was no handover of power. The President of the United States got a transition committee and two and a half months. I got my dad's notebook of suppliers and my mom's accounting books.

The lure of some fantastic month-long island Christmas celebration with Evan and cheap last-minute tickets had my parents flying out the Sunday morning after my date with Sabrina. Chester and Jill had tossed me the main set of keys to the house and the store and called themselves a cab to the airport. When I'd offered to drive them to LAX, they'd pointed out that I had the store to open.

The store.

Seven days a week. Twelve hours a day. After the cab

had taken my parents, I'd sped across Mulholland and opened Canyon Country Mart a half an hour late. Thirty-seven minutes to be exact. I knew that because Pete, probably the store's first customer when my dad's parents had opened it a million years ago, had been standing on the porch alternating tapping his watch with his finger and the floorboards with his cane.

Every moment after that had been grueling. There wasn't time to think about anything else now except the static in my ear. A burst of some annoying hold music melody started when the shop doorbell chimed as a slew of new customers came in. Phone tucked between shoulder and ear, I waved as best I could, then spoke the minute the Muzak broke and I heard a familiar voice.

"Sal, listen," I said, cutting off the string of words that would be all about catching up on my parents' travels. "The deli order got screwed up again. There's turkey and ham, but no roast beef. American, Havarti, but no Swiss."

I listened to the supplier's ready excuses, then drilled him on how he was going to fix it. Sal stopped pussy-footing around. The missing deli meat would be there in half an hour, he promised. I closed my eyes in relief. At least that would be in time for the lunch rush. The bigger issue still loomed large as the latest customers beckoned me.

The bigger issue was that Sal was going to have to go. There was no shortage of food services. Sal and Dad had been friends since my parents had taken over the store from my grandparents, but the deli guy couldn't remember orders or was losing paperwork or some even bigger problem threatened.

Sal had no son to take over that business. It was probably time for his retirement as well. If I could, I'd buy Sal a ticket to Tahiti to join my parents. All of them could spend time on a tropical beach and I could stand right here on the top of the mountain holding down the fort, maybe even add food service delivery to my already too-full plate. But Sal wasn't my dad, and what ultimately happened to our longtime supplier's deli business was another problem for another day.

The sound of paper from the fax machine curling and rustling to the floor made me look over my shoulder. I'd turned off the damned ringer an hour ago, but the lunch orders had kept coming.

After I placed my phone in the cradle, I stepped over the pile of dried tree pulp and went over to the shoppers.

One, a young woman, lifted a smoothie from the industrial fridge.

"I'm vegan and gluten-free. Can I drink this?"

The label indicated it was a virgin Bloody Mary. All the health, none of the alcohol, the marketing materials had touted. I couldn't exactly get the five-pound package of powdered smoothie base out of the back of the store to read the ingredients, ruining the illusion of fresh. So I mentally flipped through the list of additives I'd memorized for just this occasion.

"No, it has Worcestershire. I'm pretty sure there's some wheat in there. Why don't you try the kale and goji berry?"

"I'll take this one." She held up the not-gluten-free drink, her expertly manicured fingers tapping at the plastic. "That's fine. I don't eat anything green." Her statement was completely without irony.

Vegan and hated greens. That didn't leave a lot. I put on my poker face, thanking God this high-maintenance one wasn't the one I liked.

Sabrina.

That was the woman I liked.

It wasn't as if there *wasn't* some kind of hot mess going on there. But that was the hot mess I wanted the time and space to figure out. This one, the greens-hating vegan, I hoped she was a tourist with a plane ticket out of town.

"Anything else?" I asked politely not letting my face betray my thoughts.

The second woman wanted her treat to be soy-free. The third was also anti-soy, but wanted something that was low carb. I pulled a coconut cream from the back for Ms. Low Carb. With no soy-free options, I played barista and made a triple-shot cappuccino over crushed ice and almond milk. I rang them up, mostly satisfied that no one had gone away empty-handed, that I'd get paid for my troubles.

More paper curled from the fax and fell to the floor.

I looked at my watch. Where was Antonio? First on my agenda today was that I was going to make the recently hired part-time help full time. I'd planned to have that talk with my employee before the lunch rush made discussion impossible. Or now I would need an entirely new employee, because it was nearly eleven and there was no Antonio.

The phone rang. I rushed to pick it up, hoping Sal wasn't begging off with yet another excuse. But it wasn't missing meat and cheese, it was worse—it was Antonio. He was stuck behind some five-car pileup on the 210 freeway. There was no ETA in sight.

Lowering my eyelids, I tried to decide if flipping the blue and white sign to closed was the best course of action. I could call up that agent, make an appointment, sign on the dotted line of the West Hollywood net-net-net lease and be one step closer to my dream and one step further away from this nightmare.

Even more paper curled out of the fax machine and I was very close to doing just that—making a phone call and walking out the door.

The bell chimed again. I looked up, ready to figure out what in the store was organic, non-GMO, soy-free, gluten-free, and most likely flavor-free for the next hungry or thirsty Angeleno with diet restrictions.

"How can I—"

The sight of Sabrina sped up my heartbeat. The dark brown turtleneck, under her zip-front jacket comple-mented her dark eyes. Her legs were clad in some kind of cute patterned tights. I squinted a bit...were those rein-deer? It *was* December, even if it was sunny and sixty outside.

Despite looking as cute as a button, she stood there looking like she was lost at sea. The whole thing, her amazing beauty and her reticence, made me want to hug her tight and tell her everything was going to be okay.

"I...I hooked up Spencer outside, if that's okay."

I was halfway from behind the counter, wanting to pull her into a hug, when the door chime sounded and a customer came up to the counter. Prematurely abandoning Sabrina, I stepped back behind the counter, picking up the scanning gun and ringing up the purchase of a newspaper and bottle of kombucha.

Hemmed in from going to her, I said, "It's fine. Sadie loved that spot. The water bowl is under the hot dog buns," I said before turning back to prompt the man to type in his debit card pin code.

"Hi." I smiled at the next customer. Three packs of cigarettes were a super-fast transaction. Serious smokers always had exact change and their ID at the ready.

Sabrina came back shaking water from her hands where something with the hose had gone awry. She pointed to the sheaf of paper that was making a curly mound on the floor behind him.

"What's that?"

"Lunch orders."

She looked meaningfully over at the slicers and lunch prep area. "And..."

"And the new guy Antonio is stuck on the Foothill freeway for the foreseeable future."

Sabrina pulled her sweater-hoodie thing off and lifted her turtleneck over her head, revealing a soft-looking heather T. My mind was thinking about other things.

Things that would involve even fewer clothes and lots of kissing.

"Point me to the fridge," Sabrina said.

"What?" Her words did not compute. Lots of kissing and cold storage didn't go together.

"My mother could prep food for a cast of thousands in under an hour. I'll wash my hands first, though. Show me the bathroom."

I pointed the way, wondering if I were courting disaster. The fax did its thing again and more paper came out. This time there was a beep, indicating we were out of paper. I'd just filled the tray this morning. I had no idea why lunch was so all-fire popular today. But calling all those lunch recipients the last time Sal had messed up had been a nightmare I didn't care to repeat.

Gloved and all the curly blonde hair tied up in a fierce knot, Sabrina came behind the counter and picked up the pile. With amazing efficiency, she smoothed the papers and put them in a neat stack next to the machine.

"Are they timed?" she asked.

I turned my back to the store and watched her. "Timed?"

"You know, like some of these orders to be ready at eleven forty-five, others can wait until one o'clock."

I had no clue. It had been an idea on the table years ago, but my mom had said it had never been done that way. My dad had an encyclopedic knowledge of who usually ordered what and when they'd want it. That information, Chester Barnhill had not passed down.

"Not sure, check the forms."

"Gotcha." Sabrina disappeared. The door to the walk-in opened and shut. I rang up a rush of customers while she ran one slicer, then the next, making neat piles of onions, tomatoes, then meats and cheeses. Fifteen minutes later, she had a stack of orders boxed, labeled in marker with neat handwriting, and was bringing them to the walk-in.

"So what do you want me to do about the roast beef and Swiss orders? Can't find any of either."

Sal came in the door at that exact moment with the missing ingredients.

"Sal, Sabrina. Sabrina, Sal," I said before I had to go back to the caffeine, juice, and smoothie addicted.

For two long hours, we worked together like cogs in a gear. She asked few questions and learned at a laser-fast speed. Sabrina handed out sandwiches with a smile and took impromptu orders like a champ. Her poker face was a thousand times better than mine. She didn't once break into a frown over the onion-hating, sprout-loving, gluten-free-bread-needing customers who changed their minds seven different times while she was making their custom sandwiches.

She never mixed the real mayonnaise spatula with the vegan spread that served as a substitute. She even cleaned the slicer in between making the ham sandwiches and those roast beef ones for people who didn't want pork touching anything they ate. On top of that, the sandwiches I saw were beautiful, with curly green lettuce peeking from the sides. They looked like a magazine ad. She certainly had an eye for beauty.

At two o'clock, when the afternoon lull came, Sabrina lifted the logo-emblazoned cap she'd found in the office, fanning herself. It looked far cuter on her than it ever had on anyone else who'd worked at the store.

"Any more orders?"

"God no. We don't serve lunch after two. It's one of the hard and fast rules my mother insisted upon. Everyone else has to get their sandwich fix elsewhere or buy the raw ingredients from the cooler."

"That's good to hear." She untied my mother's turquoise-blue apron. "I'm exhausted. I hope Spencer doesn't have sunburn."

"When you were elbow-deep in turkey slices, I gave him Sadie's umbrella. I think all the love he got was enough to keep him going for a long while. He made a lot of friends out there."

Sabrina twisted the small silver rings on her fingers.

"What are those tiny rings?"

She stopped fiddling for a moment and looked at the middle finger on her left hand as if she didn't remember where they'd come from.

"Did you make those?"

"No. They were a gift from my mom and dad. From my whole family, really." Her voice sounded oddly resigned. Gifts were good, right? Then doubts riddled me again about what kind of relationship, if any, we were going to have.

"Are there tiny words on there," I prompted again.

"One says 'love,' another 'peace,' 'survivor,' and 'carpe diem.'" She twisted all of them so they faced upward. I could see the tiny letters stamped in each.

"What does all that mean? Are you okay?" Because after that night, I was starting to see there was something I might have missed. I walked to the door and flipped the sign to Closed. No one would die without their cans of artisanal wine cooler.

"I came here to apologize for the other night." She took the turtleneck from behind the deli counter and pulled it back on. Then she undid her hair so it fell around her shoulders.

"What do you have to be sorry for?" I was the one who should be apologizing. I was working out the way of saying exactly that, when her face crumpled. Compelled by her obvious pain, I pulled her into my arms.

"For being the worst date ever," she eventually sniffled into my shirt. "Honestly. It was a disaster. Your car. Vinegar wine. My crazypants behavior afterward."

"What particularly was crazypants?"

"Please don't make me say it," she said into my sweater. When I looked down, she turned her eyes anywhere but toward me. When she started to push away I didn't let her go.

"No, let me go. I think I need to show you something."

"I'm game."

"When that's closed, no one can come in?"

"I'll turn the lock for good measure." I went over to manipulate the dead bolt.

I nearly tripped and fell when I turned back.

She had her arms and elbows in the soft shirt and was pulling it over her head. Women getting naked was every man's fantasy, but the way she was doing it made me want to run and find a blanket to cover her up.

This was not sexy seductress. Nope, no siree. It hadn't been the other night, either, but when her head had bent toward me, my ability to say no had been severely diminished. Next thing I knew I'd had a mind-blowing orgasm and she was rushing me out the door. So I reached out and grabbed at the hem of her shirt until I could see her face.

"Sabrina, I want to get to know you better. I don't need...this...whatever you're going to do...to keep me interested."

Her arms appeared again as she pushed down the shirt, revealing a face as red as the tomatoes she'd used for sandwich garnish.

"I wasn't. Oh God, that's what you think of me? That I'm that girl who's always ready to... Jesus Christ, I do have self-esteem and some pride."

I stood paralyzed with fear of saying the wrong thing. I had wondered for a good minute or twenty if she *was* that girl. She hadn't seemed at all like that from the outset, but I really wasn't attracted to women who thought their only value to men was sex. On the other hand, I maybe did want to be with her again and didn't want to shoot myself in the foot—kill that chance dead. Though I only wanted to be with her if things were mutual, not one-way. Not like before.

I said, "I don't think you've no pride or esteem or whatever. I think you're a beautiful, talented woman who..."

"Who mortified herself last weekend. Who acted like she didn't have very much pride at all."

"Why were you going to take off your shirt?"

"There's something I want to show you. I promise, it's not the least bit sexual. But it's not something I'd like to share with the public."

As if on cue, the door rattled with someone in desperate need of juice or nicotine. I walked to the door, making sure it was still locked. Something told me I needed to finish this, whatever it was, before I started restocking and pounding away at the cash register keys.

"Closed," I called through a space through the wood blinds I'd made with my thumb and forefinger.

Cursing and muttering could be heard, but at least the dissatisfied customer walked away rather than insisting I open the door. I patted the blinds back into place, flicking lines of sun and shade across the store.

Now we could talk, but as I turned, Sabrina had her damned elbows back in the shirt, but this time she was that much closer to getting it over her head.

"Sabrina—"

Her hair stood around her in a foot-long halo of gold.

"There's something I need to tell you."

"Your hair is full of static."

She moved her hands higher and higher until they got

to the top of the golden crown of hair. Then she did that girl thing of pulling an elastic from her wrist and twisting all of her hair up in some kind of neat ponytail.

"I'm not a person to dwell on the past. I want you to know that. But the last couple of times I told a guy what I'm about to tell you, they ran for the hills. I'm giving you the chance to run. Before it hurts me too much to see you go."

"I don't scare easily, Sabrina." I threw out my arms wide. "Mulholland is already on the top of the mountain."

Her lips trembled into a kind of smile that verged on the edge of tears. The kind of watery smile people gave at funerals. She didn't look to be on the verge of death, though a lot of dead people had probably looked pretty lively the day before.

"Fair warning. You might want to tighten your laces or switch into your running shoes."

"I'm ready, I guess."

"Okay. Here goes." The elbows again, this time in a creamy white camisole that lifted slowly from her hips, over her belly button—an outie that was super cute. Then she was standing there in a bra on the top and the reindeer tights or pants or whatever women called them on the bottom. I called them the greatest invention ever. She did them proud. They clung to her slim ankles, shapely calves, strong thighs. Blood surged through me as I took in the beautiful woman standing before me. I was going to need to turn around and shift things a bit if they stood this way much longer.

With her big exhalation of breath, I tore my gaze away from her legs and looked in her eyes. They weren't brimming with tears exactly, but they weren't shining with lust, either.

I looked at her. She was normal. Two arms. Two legs. Two nicely shaped and sized breasts. The lacy bra wasn't see-through, but it did spark my imagination, so I shifted my eyes away from that. She had some kind of sparkly things in her ears. It matched the pendant hanging below her bra. I shifted my thighs uncomfortably in my soft corduroy pants. They were my most comfortable winter pants, but they were chafing a bit now. Had the blood surge rendered me so dumb I couldn't see what was supposed to be obvious?

"Closed," I shouted over my shoulder toward the door as it rattled another time.

"When are you open?" came the question reply.

"About an hour," I said. I hoped that was enough time for us to finish the conversation we were about to have. Because this show needed some tell.

There was a subsequent rattle, but it stopped as abruptly as it began.

"So..."

"I'm really sorry to have to say this—"

"I knew it." She bent to the floor and started gathering heaps of clothes...tank, turtleneck.

I strode over, plucked the clothes from her hand. "I don't understand what's going on here. You're half naked, but I'm sorry to say I'm still very confused."

"Don't you see it?" she whispered as if there were a second head, or third eye, or fifth limb.

"Please tell me what you want me to see," I whispered.

She stood tall on the scuffed oak floor. I followed suit and stood back a few inches, trying to bring parts of her into focus. Slowly, she traced a finger to a spot just above her bra. I followed its inevitable move down between her bra cups and to her flat stomach.

I concentrated, then I saw it. A long, thin scar.

"What happened?" The question needed no further clarification.

"Open-heart surgery." Her tone was matter of fact, almost mechanical, now that the issue was on the table, so to speak.

"Wow." Of all the things I'd have guessed, some kind of quadruple bypass or the like wouldn't have been it. "You're how old? Twenty-nine, right?"

"Bicuspid aortic valve disorder, is what it's called. It's genetic—from my father's side. He lost his mom and aunt when he was a kid. When I was a kid, the doctors heard a murmur. But lots of kids have murmurs, so you know, no one really thought about it, including my dad, who I think blocked it out. Or maybe they didn't really know those things in First Nations communities."

"Why did you have surgery, though?" I asked. "I've known people with murmurs, none have had anything like this."

"When I was in my first year at university, I was at some weekend fair in London, the Ontario one. I was riding a fake bronco when I lost my breath. I couldn't get it back. My friends had to find a hospital. My parents had to leave my brother and sister and get on a plane to Toronto. That's when I got the diagnosis."

"The aortic valve disorder."

"Bicuspid, then the rest. But yeah. It was what had caused the murmur. But it was worse than your garden-variety murmur. Much worse. The doctors said that I couldn't leave the hospital until I had surgery to correct the defect."

"I'm sorry."

"We had two choices. Or one, rather. A valve replacement. Either pig or cow or mechanical."

"What does all that mean?" I'd never much thought about doctors or hospitals or medical care. My mom took care of my dad's stuff. The city was full of hospitals, though. It couldn't be only old people who got sick.

"They cracked open my chest and took out the defective part and put in a titanium part. It should last the rest of my life."

"So you're not dying?"

"Gosh, no."

I sighed. That was good to hear. For a long second, I'd thought this confessional may be going in an entirely different direction.

"Do you have to do something different? I mean, would you have a heart attack if you had sex?" I stepped back a bit. "Not that I'm presuming anything. I'm just trying to understand."

Understand what in the hell had happened the other night. Not that it had been entirely unpleasant, but sex, like everything else in a relationship, should be a two-way street.

"I have to take blood thinners. I should probably tell you that. So if I hurt myself, I may need to be rushed to Cedars or Providence Saint Joseph, so they can induce clotting. Otherwise, I'm fine."

"Now, which part is supposed to send me running?" I was able to ask this now that my heart had calmed down. Now that I knew there was no third shoe to drop.

"Are you making fun of me?"

"No. I'm seriously asking."

"Do you not see the scar? It's...it's really...hideous."

"It's just a scar, Sabrina. We all have them."

"Not twenty-two centimeters in the middle of your chest."

"Does that mean you thought I wouldn't find you attractive if I saw it?"

"It's nine inches. That's what I think it is in inches, nine."

"So what, your master plan was to get me so hot and bothered that I can't muster up the energy to give you the same pleasure, then you hustle me out the door?"

She didn't breathe a word, but the flicker in her eyes told me that's exactly what the plan had been.

I took one step toward Sabrina. She took a mincing step back. I took one more step, then another, then one last. Until I was inches from Sabrina and she had her back up against the Mexican food shelves. Jars of salsa and cans of black and refried beans rattled against the wood. I braced my hands against the shelves. The rattling stopped.

She looked like a deer on Beverly Glen caught in the headlights of my new SUV. I liked her big sexy brown eyes, but not startled. I wanted them a little bit foggy, like they'd been the other night on her purple couch before it had all gone sideways.

The only way I knew to achieve that foggy look was to lean in a little bit closer. Her eyelids drooped. A little closer. They closed all the way. Her lips parted as she took in a breath.

I pressed my mouth against those parted lips slick with some kind of fruity-smelling gloss. She let her breath out and I caught it. Sweet like raspberries. I moved closer until our chests and thighs touched.

There was nothing hotter than a woman in a bra. I changed the angle of our kiss, fit my hands against the sides of her waist. Warm, soft, woman flesh filled my palms, made the pads on the tips of my fingers tingle. When my hands moved up her sides, her breath quickened. I licked her bottom lip, and she quivered just the tiniest bit.

She was so responsive. It was turning me on more than it should in the middle of my parents' store. Even though I knew better, I moved my right hand just that much higher and that bit to the left so that my entire palm covered bra cup. Warm flesh pushed behind that scrap of nylon against my hand.

Sabrina pulled her head back, separating them by inches. "Do you want some time to think about all this?"

I traced a single finger from the bottom of her scar, the tiny line bumpy under my finger, to the bottom of her bra. Distracted, I traced the top of one cup, then the other.

"Henry..."

"I'm a guy. You're really sexy." My finger swayed from its path arching, straining toward the hard nipple I knew was waiting for me underneath. "But um, I'm not putting on different shoes."

"What...shoes?" It took a long minute for her to get the question out. She looked nearly as dazed and out of breath as I was.

"I'm not running away, Sabrina, by any means. But I have to open the door now before someone calls in a hostage situation to LAPD."

"Hostage?"

"Mom and Dad got a little frisky once. Cops were chasing a home invader. Somehow the store being locked in the middle of the day and a neighborhood search for a criminal got conflated."

A kind half smile broke out on her face. It was the most positive emotion I'd seen out of her in hours. "No lights and sirens."

"I'm right here, Sabrina. I really like you; if you're into exploring this, I'm in. Now can you please put on your three shirts? Or at least two. Because while I really like you without that tank thing and your turtleneck, I think it may confuse the customers just a bit."

"It's a camisole, it helps cover..." she said.

"There's no need to ever cover yourself around me." Less was always better as far as I was concerned.

I made sure we were both decent before I opened the shade and propped open the door to the public. I batted away the weird proprietary feelings I had about her nudity, turning my attention back to business.

After the ten people who'd been cooling their heels on the porch came in, I poked my head out. Spencer stood, his tail wagging in excitement. I turned when I felt Sabrina's presence next to me. She had on all her clothes and plus a bulky sweater she'd come up the hill in.

"Going home?"

"Do you need me to stay and help?"

"No...no. Antonio's parking now. That's his pickup pulling into the lot." I'd never been so disappointed to see someone I'd have sold a kidney for earlier.

"I'll hike home, then. Do the rest of my workout."

"Did you have a cardiologist clear your trip?" It came to me all at once, the danger she could face if she climbed Kilimanjaro. "'Cause what if something happens to you on the side of the mountain? Do they have adequate hospitals there?"

"Please. Not this. Not now. You sound like my parents. They don't want me to so much as ride a bike without medical clearance."

"I'm sure it's because they love you."

Someone rang the little bell on the counter. The one for when no one was in the store proper. When I didn't come back in right away, it jingled again. This time louder.

"I assumed you of all people would know what it's like to be on the receiving end of a little too much love." Her gaze at me was pointed.

Before I could come up with the right response, Antonio was at the steps, excuses tripping from his mouth. Sabrina had unwound the dog and the bell was ringing mercilessly. So I let her go, even though the discussion was just beginning and far from over.

And I went into the store my parents had gifted me. Yeah, I understood her all right, knew that love sometimes came with too many strings.

Chapter Nine

"THANKS FOR GIVING IT ANOTHER GO." I opened the gate wide enough to let Henry in, but narrow enough to keep Spencer from running out. "Down, boy," I called when the Rhodesian ridgeback made the doggy-like decision to try to jump on my guest.

"It's okay." Henry patted the dog after it sat obediently. He hefted a zipped canvas bag bearing the Canyon Country Mart logo. "I brought the drinks."

"Come on in." I started to close the front door behind him.

"You're going to leave Spencer out?"

"He loves to sniff around. I'll keep an eye on him," I said. It *was* partially for the dog's benefit. Spencer did love to investigate the garden. But I also wanted a minute where it could be only the two of us without a wiggly, needy creature in between. "The minute he starts to dig up the landscaping, I'll call him in."

Firmly, I pushed the door closed. Turning away, I resisted the urge to take a moment to pump my fist in the air. I'd set out a Henry-sized plan and executed it.

Called him.

Apologized *again* for the crazy.

Invited him out—well, in—for a make-up date.

Here he was. All handsome in white jeans and black shirt and leather jacket stretched across broad shoulders and what I knew to be delicious abs. That and black zip boots. He knew how to dress to emphasize his wide, sculpted chest and long, lean legs.

"Where can I put this?" He hefted his bag higher, partially obscuring the view of his torso and breaking my stare.

"Oh, wine! In the fridge, or I can get you ice if the fridge is too cold," I said, discomfited that I didn't have the right equipment for wine and spirits. "I don't own one of those fancy temperature-controlled, smoked-glass things that everyone else seems to have."

"Just point me toward the kitchen and I'll be fine. If conditions always had to be perfect, no one would drink wine." His statement of something that obvious was oddly comforting.

Wrapping my hand on his hard biceps was no mistake. I took the opportunity to touch him like I'd been craving and also steered him in the right direction. Then I reluctantly let him go. Henry disappeared in the kitchen. I unmuted the television and turned to one of the popular music stations.

My triumphant good mood took over my body and I danced a little jig of happiness. Kind of like when I was a kid and my mom had me and my brother and sister dance the wiggles out.

"The dancing has started already?" Henry's deep voice penetrated through the bumping beat music.

I whirled around, kind of embarrassed to be caught with my guard down. "Did you tiptoe?"

"I maybe heard some music. Didn't want to miss the opportunity for a dance party."

I turned the music louder with the TV remote. I grabbed his hands.

"C'mon, baby..." I sang with the music. I swayed, but moving him was like trying to dance with a brick wall. Ha, he wasn't ready to let his guard down. Henry sidestepped awkwardly, shuffling more than dancing.

"I, um, don't really dance," he protested.

"What?" I didn't believe him, not with those hips. Like most men, he was probably a little too wound up to let loose. "You can't invoke the words dance party but not, you know, dance."

"The music's a little fast for me," he admitted. "I've only done the mosh pit."

He was a wealth of surprises. Not for the first time, I recalibrated my opinion of him.

"Like metal concerts?" I asked.

"More alternative. The best concert ever was The Killers. Opened for Morrissey at the Wiltern. Incubus was great too. That's a lot of jumping up and down, though.

None of that hip movement you were doing when I came in."

I thought he probably had a lot of great hip movement. I was counting on it, in fact, but steered my mind from the bedroom and came back to the present conversation.

"Oh my God. You sound like my friends from Vancouver. Did you have long hair and wear black t-shirts?"

"Guilty as charged."

"Wow. That I wish I'd seen. You were probably super cute then all broody and in black." I let go of his hands and cupped my own over my mouth and stopped swaying. "Not that you aren't cute now. You're way more hot than cute, though." My stomach roiled with mortification, not to mention the heat that was making the stupid fire I'd started in the fireplace completely superfluous. What was it about him that made me blurt out my thoughts before I could sensor them?

Henry stopped dead still and oh so slowly shed this leather jacket. If his face wasn't lit with the most gorgeous half smile I'd ever seen, I wouldn't have known that he was trying to get me worked up with his little impromptu striptease.

Casually, he tossed the jacket on the couch. "You said this was an awards-viewing party? The Golden Globes are January and Oscars February. So what's tonight?"

"Critics' Choice."

He nodded his recognition. "Are you a big movie buff?" he asked.

"Not at all. Television is okay, though I watch mostly

dramas."

"So the party?"

I cringed at his use of the term. Had I said the word party when I'd texted him? Successfully, I battled the urge to check my phone to see what I'd typed when I'd worked up the courage, well past my bedtime, to invite him back for what I hoped was not a repeat performance of our first date, but an opportunity to see I was a normal woman who didn't ambush men's cocks with my mouth.

"It's a party of two. That's okay, right?" I hated the little squeak of unsureness in my voice.

"More than okay, Sabrina." His own was calm, deep, and sure. It sent shivers of anticipation up and down my spine.

"Mina Foy is up for Best Actress in a Movie Made for Television or Limited Series."

His eyebrows shot up. "Amazing that you got that one in a single try."

"Been practicing for days. Had to type it like a million times as I'm updating my resume and website."

"Looking for a new job?"

"No. Kind of. I like doing individual pieces, and I'll always continue doing that. But I'd like to have a bit of a wider reach. I'm going to submit my portfolio to some jewelry stores and see if I can have my own line."

"That's amazing. The Sabrina Lynch line?"

"Not the eponymous type. My business is called Severn Gael. It's Gaelic. Celtic, really."

"Very cool. And Mina Foy is wearing a Severn Gael

original."

"She is." I pressed a few buttons and a large digital clock appeared on the screen. "Is it okay if I turn to the channel? I want to see the red carpet."

"It's blue."

I muted the too-loud commercial. "Blue?"

"Critics' Choice Awards has blue carpet. It's their way of standing out during the awards season." The screen flashed and several entertainment reporters crowded the screen as they stood around a very long, very blue rug.

Color me surprised at his knowledge of that little detail. "How do you know all this?"

"Way more years in Los Angeles under my belt," he said, his words sort of cryptic.

Now I was back to worrying about the mama's boy thing again. Had he and his mom shared champagne and popcorn during awards season? The thought was kind of heartwarming.

Henry started toward the kitchen he'd abandoned for the impromptu dance. "The awards are going to start soon; do you mind if I go get the drinks ready?"

"Ahhh. The food. All the dancing and I forgot the food." I ran to the kitchen, expecting billowing smoke. I threw open the oven, but only heat, not smoke, enveloped my already hot head. I peered in at the baking sheets. My appetizers were a little brown, but not too bad. Still edible, thank goodness. One more disaster averted. We were like our own version of Murphy's Law.

"Hogs in a blanket." I pulled out the pan and, with

mincing fingers, added the phyllo-wrapped Andouille sausage to the large platter balanced on the counter.

"Is that a...repurposed...hub cap?" he asked, eyeing the precariously balanced metal serving dish.

"It's Mona's. She does art from reclaimed objects. It's a statement about California and recycling and something else I should remember. But I don't. It's great for entertaining, though."

"What else you got?" He looked famished. Was working in a store like being a cobbler's kid? Surrounded by a lot of food he didn't eat?

"Salmon caviar sushi bites, mini blini napoleons, and crispy corn tortillas with chicken and cheddar."

"Wow, okay. You do not play around." He gestured vaguely toward the fridge. "I think I've got it covered."

"Can you bring this in?" I handed over the platter when the sound of red-carpet host Tiera Tenley's voice came from the living room. "I've got to run back and see..."

Henry was laying the platter on the table when Mina Foy made her entrance.

"Is that yours?" He pointed at the actress with Tiera's microphone under her nose.

"Not anymore," I joked. "But yeah, I designed it. It's...shhhh."

On the screen, the glammed-up TV reporter pushed the microphone as far as possible into Mina's face. "You look fabulous tonight. Who did your gown?"

"Thanks so much, Tiera. The gown is from Dolce and Gabbana. The shoes are Jimmy Choo, of course. The jewelry is by a new up-and-coming designer right here in L.A., Sabrina Lynch of Severn Gael."

"That's an interesting piece. Diamonds?"

"Not diamonds, Tiera. I was born in Angola while my parents were in the Peace Corps. I have a special place in my heart for the people of Western Africa. I refuse to wear blood diamonds from conflict areas. Sabrina Lynch heard my concerns and did a wonderful job weaving semi-precious stones that highlight the Swarovski crystal teardrop pendant Elton Lamb gave me after our last movie wrapped."

"Thanks, Mina. We wish you luck tonight," Tiera Tenley said as the camera zoomed back in on the reporter.

I muted the set. I couldn't resist jumping up and down, clapping my hands like a gleeful child. "Oh my God. That was the best endorsement ever! I've gotta get a clip of that to add to my website."

"Congratulations," Henry said, his voice resonating somewhere deep inside me. "I think a toast is in order."

He handed me a crystal flute that he must have found at the way back of my cabinet. I only had three of the four in the set, so I'd hidden them away, hoping the friends who'd given them to me as a housewarming gift wouldn't know that I'd been so careless. I'd dropped and broke one of them right out of the box.

"What's this?" It was something sparkly and golden, but I didn't want to guess champagne. My conjecture was that there were probably thousands of yellow fizzy wines. He probably knew the names of them all.

"Champagne cocktail with lemon twist."

I took a large sip. "This is delicious. What's that red thing fizzing in the bottom?"

"Angostura bitters-infused sugar cube."

"I'm going to pretend I'm sophisticated enough to know what that is."

I finished the drink and went back to the kitchen for napkins and toothpicks. Through the rest of the blue carpet spiel, we ate and drank while talking about what we liked in movies. He liked action, but we both appreciated historical and drama.

"Really good." He wiped his hands with a napkin after he ate the last appetizer. He swallowed the last of the champagne. "We make a good team."

"I know, right? I love tiny food. It's kind of weird to make lots of appetizers for only one person. But with you here brining the wine and champagne. It makes a tray of cheese puffs okay."

He hefted the empty platter.

"You don't have to do that."

"My mother trained me well," he said and winked. Relief and his taking my earlier faux pas about his mother in stride made me weak with laughter.

"Are you doing any more award show jewelry?" he asked when he came back in the room, two sparkling waters in hand.

"One for the Oscars and one for the Golden Globes." I was super proud to have nearly achieved my goals. This was the second to last step of my before-thirty plan.

"Do you always watch from home?"

My hair fluttered from his breath. Henry was much closer to me on the couch than before. Even with the centimeters between us, heat from his leg seemed to leap to mine.

"I don't rate for a ticket."

He rubbed his hands along his thigh, once, then twice. Leaning forward, his knees turned toward me, he said, "Would you be my date for the Oscars?"

Butterflies, bees, and every other flying thing took flight inside me. "Are you kidding me?"

I threw my arms around his neck for an impromptu hug. My heart leapt at the close contact. His cologne was woodsy and subtle. I pulled back when his voice rumbled in his chest.

"My mother gets two tickets every year. They won't be flying back from the South Pacific. You could see your creations in person."

Grabbing his surprisingly soft scruff, I placed a quick kiss on his nose. "I think that is really cool."

The show came back from commercial, and two actors I didn't know came up on stage. Mina Foy's category flashed on screen behind them.

Scooting across the couch cushion, I turned to the screen. "I want to see this."

"The nominees for Best Actress in a Movie Made for Television or Limited Series are..." They alternately rattled off six names, the last of which was Mina Foy. The actors made some joke about tearing open the thick paper that held the winner's name. Finally, one wrestled the folded card from the other and opened it. "The Critics' Choice is Mina Foy!" he announced.

I was out of my seat like I'd won the award. The camera immediately zoomed in on Mina in her black velvet dress with its plunging neckline. The crystal that had been right in my studio upstairs only weeks earlier sparkled in the light of the airplane hangar. Mina stood and hugged the other people at her table, some of whom had been in the TV movie's vignettes with her.

Mina Foy had her hands up to her face, then wiped away tears of joy as she strode confidently onstage. The actress pulled first one presenter then the other into a tight hug. With the huge doorknob-shaped award in one hand, she approached the microphone.

"Wow. I don't have much time. I want to thank my family and friends for your support over the years. Also, Elton Lamb, Elton Lamb, Elton Lamb. Like you've done for so many other women, you've changed my—"

A large "oh" reverberated through the hangar as Mina Foy's necklace self-destructed.

The slow-motion play of crystals bouncing on stage was probably in my head. It could only have been one or two seconds in real time. Closing my eyes against the spectacle didn't stop the pain that burst through my head like flashes of lights behind my lids. It was as if a vise were squeezing my temples. Fruitlessly, I massaged the side of my head with my fingers. Then I pressed those same fingers against my closed eyelids.

I couldn't bear to look.

It couldn't be happening again.

No one. Not one single other person in the world had this much bad luck.

I hadn't realized my head had hit my knees until Henry's large hand came to rest on the small of my back, then traveled up slowly to squeeze my shoulder.

Sucking in air and trying to prop up my courage, I levered myself up and leaned against the back of the couch. I opened one lid, then the other.

Mina was standing onstage, what remained of the crystal necklace in her hand as a woman in an emerald-green sequined gown helped the actress disappear stage left behind the blue curtains. Seconds later, a commercial for Henry's SUV filled the screen, the big steel behemoth driving down an empty Malibu road.

The tone that indicated I was receiving a text message on my phone beeped once, then again, then again.

I looked at the phone face go light, then dark, then light again on the side table. I didn't even bother reaching for it. I already knew what it would say. What all the texts would say. Some version of "sorry" and "too bad" and probably one or two "you got too big for your britches" types. Not everyone who had my phone number was nice.

Turning to Henry, I said, "I think I won't be needing those tickets for the Academy Awards." I wasn't sure I was ready to show my face at the Oscars. Not unless I could duck through a back door and remain hidden most of the night.

"This happened before, right?"

"You saw the necklace at the restaurant. That's for the Golden Globes. Then there was Gemma Hart. I'm totally, totally screwed. It's my fault, but I can't fix it... Third time is NOT a charm, despite what everyone says."

The landline phone started ringing before I could finish feeling sorry for myself. Into the cordless receiver, I explained to Mona then two other friends I'd begged to watch the show that I had no idea the cause of the problem. When my parents' names popped up on the caller ID, I muted the ringer.

"Are you okay?" Henry asked. He pulled at his sweater, shifted a bit on the couch.

"I'm mortified. Horribly, horribly mortified. The big plug she gave me was great. But now it's like a beacon of who *not* to hire."

Henry rubbed at the space between my shoulder blades. "Maybe it's something simple..."

"What kind of designer am I where the jewelry keeps falling to bits? This was going to be my year. I pitched dozens of agents and managers to accessorize their clients. I spent all fall working on designs, finding unique gems, custom-crafting each piece. And then this. Never before has this happened. I've been doing the same thing for ten years and it's like I'm back in year one. What am I going to do?" I hoped the last hadn't come out as a wail or a whine.

I felt a bit cold and lonely when he stopped rubbing my back. Henry stood, clearing out the plates and glasses.

When he came back, he said, "Maybe I can help you.

Sometimes putting two heads together can be better than one."

"I've been over this a hundred times."

"Let's try for one hundred and one."

"Why don't you come see my etchings?" I'd meant it as a joke to relieve the tension.

Kind of.

Sort of.

Maybe.

Maybe not.

There were so many emotions swirling through me that I wasn't sure what was going to happen with Henry, with my jewelry, with my heart. The jewelry, though, I didn't want to think about. I had a good idea what we could do for distraction...

Henry must have had the same idea when he pulled me in for a kiss. He'd probably meant it to be short. I had certainly thought it was going to be short. The distraction, though, was too good to ignore. His lips didn't speak words of recrimination or pity. Instead, they gave me what I needed exactly at that moment...solace, strength.

I grasped the fingers of his left hand with those of my right. Gratified he didn't flinch at the roughened tips of my fingers, I pulled him up the stairs that curved first one way, then the other. When I could have, should have, gone right, I turned left. Pushed opened the door. Waited for his reaction.

"This is not the studio."

"You're an astute one, Henry. I, uh, need to not talk

about red carpets or blue carpets or Hollywood right now. I need you, just you."

I stared into his blue-blue eyes, the color of the clear California sky. I was fighting some kind of war within himself. When his pupils widened with desire, I knew instantly what his decision would be. Pleased, I blew out the breath I hadn't known I was holding.

"It's very purple in here," he said. He walked toward the bed and smoothed his fingers against the velvet duvet, the color of my favorite stone.

"Amethyst is my favorite semi-precious gem. It's the first faceted stone I remember seeing as a kid. It's what made me interested in jewelry. I love the idea of designing something that allows people to wear beautiful stones that come from the earth."

"That's very cool. You're very cool, Miss Sabrina Lynch. Don't let anyone tell you otherwise."

Henry sat on the duvet. First he unzipped one ankle-high boot, then the other. Black socks came off next. His naked feet were straight and narrow and nice. Oddly nice. That tiniest bit of vulnerability of his toes floored me. I'd seen the most private part of him, but this was more intimate somehow.

I sat beside him, turned my back to him and lifted my hair.

"Can you unzip this for me?"

"Where? How?" I shivered as his hands grazed my neck.

"There's a tiny pull tab near the top."

Henry rubbed my neck. I leaned forward, letting his hands warm me, calm me. "That feels really good."

"You're tense. I mean, I get it. But there are a couple of knots back here." He found the zipper in the black beaded top and eased the teeth apart slowly. Gooseflesh rose on my arms and chest.

"Cold? I can fix that." Scorching-hot lips along the bumps of my spine chased away the chill. And just like that my nerve endings were on fire.

I stood and shimmied the jumpsuit off my arms, and down my hips and legs. It pooled on the floor in a heap of beads, sequins, and silk.

"That's one piece. I had no idea."

I turned toward him in my camisole and purple bikini panties. He ran a finger under the lace of my waistband. "It's a theme."

One knee came down by his left hip. I straddled him, pinning my knee on the other side. Kissing, touching, that's what I wanted right now, not thinking or talking. I slipped both hands under the front of his shirt, and the soft fabric lifted from his flat belly, hard chest. Henry lifted his arms and the shirt was gone.

Suddenly years of deprivation and half measures weren't enough.

"I want more, Henry," I gasped.

"More what?"

"More everything."

My hand on his jaw brought him closer, narrowed the gap between us. It started with one kiss that sizzled all the way down to my purple toenails. I laid a hand against his neck and pulled him infinitely closer, slipping my tongue into his mouth, his taste bittersweet like mine. The whiskers brushing against my mouth and cheek were rough against smooth. The contrast between us heated my blood.

We kissed for what seemed like hours, first slanting our mouths one way, then the other. I traced my fingers along his cheek, jaw, and neck, feeling for the pulse there. He tucked my hair behind one ear, then the other, his fingers outlining the rim of my ear. His index fingers whispered against the sensitive spots just behind my lobes. Shivers went down my spine. The kiss went on and on before I finally broke away.

Two hands at my hips, he lifted me and slipped off my panties. "Purple panties have to go," he said before lying back down on my bed. I leaned down to kiss him, but he put a finger to my lips. His fingers gripped my naked hips and brought my most secret place up to his face. At the first tentative flick of his tongue, I nearly shot to the stratosphere. Fortunately, my hand came up and kept my head from hitting the slanted ceiling beams that hung low over the top of my head.

"Jesus, Henry."

"Shh. Let me..." He didn't say anything more. Instead, I grabbed on to the slatted white bed frame and held on for dear life. It was all I could do, just take the pleasure. He held me tight, and I couldn't unbuckle his pants, take the focus from me, as much as I wanted to do that. Turn the focus on him.

Thoughts about anything other than my pleasure left me then. Each expert flick of his tongue brought me closer to the brink, closer to the oblivion of orgasm, but not to completion. It was so good, the magic Henry was making with his tongue, but I couldn't stop myself from holding back. Something like fear chased the lust away.

Henry's hands, as if sensing my withdrawal, eased me back so I was straddling his chest. His hand left my hip long enough to lift my camisole from my waist and over my belly button.

Involuntarily, I flinched.

"What's wrong?"

As if what was wrong wasn't the most obvious thing in the world. Everything was wrong with me. I was living on borrowed time. I wasn't whole, perfect. I made mistakes.

"I never take off my camisole in front of anyone." It was what I could admit to aloud.

"You took it off in the middle of my store."

"Yeah, there was that." I turned my head to the side. Toward the single purple accent wall, looking at the flock of doves I'd painstakingly painted over a long American holiday weekend.

"Sabrina?" The sound of my name pulled my gaze toward him again. "Do you trust me?"

I nodded because I did. He'd been nothing but honest and kind. "Then trust that I like you. Trust that I'm here of my free will after I've already seen the part of you that you like to keep hidden."

We'd been intimate in one of the closest ways that a

man and woman could, not just that first night, but even moments ago.

A little frisson of excitement rippled through my body. I wanted him. I was going to have to give up something to get him. Exhaling, I closed my eyes then lifted the top. Henry must have helped me, because one minute it was wound around my arms and the next minute I was free.

By reflex, my arms moved to cross my chest like a corpse in a coffin. Not that I was dead. Far from the edge of it, like I'd been on before open-heart surgery. In fact, I felt more alive right now than I ever had.

With life, though, came embarrassment, fear, trepidation. All pooled in my belly, pushing out the arousal that had been there moments ago. This seesaw between life and death, arousal and embarrassment was hard, maybe harder than I thought it would ever be. This was the reason I'd shunned intimacy, because the price, for me, was very high.

"Where are you?"

Henry's voice intruded on my thoughts. Brought me back to having my very exposed, nude bottom half straddling his half-dressed body. How did I get from here to where I wanted to be?

"Sorry, I'm shit at this."

"Don't be sorry. Be here. With me." His blue eyes were direct and clear.

"What do you mean?"

"Please don't go to that place you went before, where

you think feelings can't touch you. I'm here with you because there's nowhere else I want to be."

"Oh, Henry..."

"Now there's a joke I've heard a time or two."

I tried to cover it up, but I couldn't. Laughter started in my belly and pushed its way up through my lungs and finally out of my mouth. I clapped my hands over my lips to keep it inside, but it was no use.

Henry sat up and flipped me so I was lying on my back. Gently, he placed a kiss along every centimeter of my scar. When I thought I couldn't stand his scrutiny one minute longer, his deft fingers flicked open my bra hooks and in a moment, the scrap of nylon and lace floated to the floor, far out of reach.

"Damn."

"What?" I looked down and around, worried that something else had gone awry.

"You're amazingly beautiful is what. I mean, under all those high-necked shirts that go clear down to your waist, all this was hiding underneath. I had no idea."

"You thought about that?"

"I've been thinking about that for months. You're beautiful. How could I not notice you?"

"Why didn't you ever say anything?"

"For the past few years I've been away long stretches of time, in Italy, in France, Germany—then in Napa and the Pacific Northwest. Dating for short stretches of time is not what I'm interested in. I'm looking for something far more long term."

My brain knew we were having a serious conversation. Some kind of response was expected of me. But for the life of me, I couldn't figure out what to say. Instead, I found myself biting my lip as a wave of pure pleasure rippled through my body. I was working up to getting sound and vibration from my body to speak when his fingers brushed my nipples like he was strumming an acoustic guitar.

That brief touch was like a shock of lightning to my core. With that touch, I was aroused again, slickness easing the friction of my thighs rubbing together like two sticks trying to start a fire.

With laser focus, he took one straining nipple between his lips. Heat, wetness, and the brush of beard made my hips shoot off the bed. His own hips were the only thing between me and the stratosphere. The cold leather of his belt and the colder brass of his buckle pressed against my heated skin. Vulnerable, I raked him with my eyes.

"I'm the only one naked," I whispered, unable and not really wanting to mask the longing in my voice.

Damn the mouth that said that.

The fingers that had made music with my body were now curled around the leather and brass circling his waist. I didn't know if he was being slow to tease me or if he was moving like honey from a jar because his own coordination was shot. Either way, I wanted his black belt and white pants and his underwear gone. I licked my lips in anticipation, my eyes stayed glued to the belt, its unhooking, the breath of air that came with leather clearing belt loops,

Henry coiling it before dropping it over the side of the mattress.

Not caring that I was gawking, I waited for Henry to get to the button and zipper that would get him that much closer to nude. But his hands were back on my skin, having abandoned his own clothes, one pinching and soothing a nipple in equal measure. The other cupping the back of my head, pulling me in for a kiss.

I made no move to hold back this time. I sank into his mouth, enjoying the feel of his lips on mine, the pleasure of our tongues mating. Skin met glorious skin. Coarse curly hairs created a sensuous friction against my breasts. I traced his biceps and triceps, the muscles hard under hot skin.

The moan that rumbled through his chest told me that he was as far gone as me, maybe more so, because I had enough rational thought left to know that I wanted those pants gone. It couldn't be that he was shy, so I untangled my hands from his arms and put one on either side of the placket.

Henry's "no" as he unsealed his mouth from mine was emphatic.

"Why not? Don't you want to?" Because maybe he didn't. All the trepidation and insecurity that I thought I'd kept at bay came back with a wallop.

"Of course. But I want to go slow this time, make sure you don't try to distract me like last time."

"I didn't—"

"Sabrina, that was some world-class deflection. Not.

This. Time." Each of his last three words was punctuated with a kiss on a different part of my face—her brow, cheek, and chin.

Nerves of a different kind set in, so I deflected with kisses and well-placed fingers on a sensitive spot on his neck that made him shiver time and again. Henry was far cleverer than I'd given him credit for, though. After a few minutes of my ministrations and him nearly losing control, he pinned my wrists above my head with a single hand, then went to work.

He traced a path down the sensitive underside of my arms, through the crooks of my elbows, briefly touching on my underarms. The slight tickle was torture of a wholly different kind. The assault on my senses continued. This time he replaced his roving hand with devious lips. He kissed my eyelids, the bridge of my nose, skipping my lips to land at the hollow of my neck. His tongue took over as it ran from one pebbled nipple then the other, going lower, then lower still until he was at my folds again. His hand let my wrists go, and the thrust of my fingers in his hair urged him on as my arousal wound me tighter than a spring.

Every thought and fear was drummed from my head by the blood pounding in my veins. Henry continued to do magical things with his tongue against my clitoris until I thought I was going to die. News of my death was greatly exaggerated. Instead, on a single exhalation, a loud moan left me and my sex pulsed with release.

Wide smile in place, Henry came back up to lie at my side. There was so much I wanted to say, but I was well out of breath. Just when I was able to form a coherent thought, Henry rose above me, naked finally. His thick engorged cock was fully sheathed to protect us both.

"Are you ready?" he whispered in my ear as the underside of his penis nudged gently at my clit. As the arousal started tightening in me again, I could only nod. Fisting himself, he notched against my opening and filled me inch by glorious inch.

If pressed, I might have admitted that I was a size queen. I cared not only about the motion of the boat, but the size as well. Henry was a yacht by any standard. That full feeling of him thrusting against the opening to my womb felt amazing again and again and again. If I could have made it go on forever, I would, but I wasn't able to hold out. My second orgasm came on like a wave taking me totally by surprise.

I'd long ago lost the ability to hold myself back to try to be quiet. And I was glad of it, because when I opened my eyes, his looked lit with a flame that burned brighter with each cry that came from my lips.

Now that I wasn't overwhelmed with pleasure, I focused on wringing it from him. I squeezed Henry from the inside and gave a little swivel to my hips. With that small movement, he lost control of his measured rhythm and came with three powerful thrusts.

Spent, I watched the shadows flicker in the room as wind blew the trees, filtering light from the moonlit sky.

"Where's the bathroom?"

"First door on the left."

Lethargic, he rose from my duvet.

From the pillow embroidered with *"fais de beaux rêves,"* I extracted my nightshirt and covered my body with it. In the quiet, I could hear my artificial valve clicking. God, I hoped it hadn't been beating like a crazy metronome during sex.

Naked and unselfconscious, Henry came back cleaned up. He dug around the floor for his boxers and pulled the red and black checked fabric up to cover himself. When he lay back on the bed, he threw his arms above his head and closed his eyes.

Unobserved, I took him in. All beautiful six feet of him. I'd have loved to study him completely nude, but I didn't have the guts to ask him to remove the briefs he'd just put on.

"*Le petit mort*," I whispered.

"Little death?"

"It's what the French sometimes say after sex." I shut up because who in the hell knew what I was trying to say. I wanted to say thank you, and thank God that I wasn't permanently broken. That vigorous sex wouldn't kill me nor was I repellant to good-looking men. That I'd like to slip my hands through the placket of his boxers and see, now that I could focus, if the light smattering of freckles across his body continued there. Instead, I lay back and let him gather me in his embrace.

"You'll figure it out," he said.

Silently, I sent up a prayer of thanks that someone still had faith in me. He made me almost believe it.

Chapter Ten

SABRINA AND SPENCER had taken to showing up nearly every morning for the last week. She came at the perfect time, right between the morning coffee rush and the lunch sandwich hustle. If I could spare a minute, I'd have a smoothie while she had coffee.

She'd hinted more than once about a third date. I'd felt like an ass for not being able to answer her in the affirmative or even commit to a day of the week. More and more, I started to appreciate how much work my parents had done. They may not have taken my suggestions, but before they left I could come and go as I pleased. Their presence assured that I could go out at night, or on weekends, or spend weeks abroad furthering my training in far-flung vineyards. I was wistful for what West Hollywood could have been, and what Alsace and Burgundy had been.

Dutifully, I took the next customer. Took her money and handed over her cookies.

At ten forty-five precisely, I heard Sabrina dump her doggie poo bag in the outside garbage. In a few seconds, she'd ask if she could wash her hands in the back. I pushed espresso beans into the grinder, then tamped them down in the porta-filter. Hazelnut half and half was in the front of the fridge, as she liked it better than milk or soy, almond, coconut, or all the other choices I needed to have on hand for my customers.

"Morning." I nodded to her. Purposefully taciturn, I held in everything else. My feelings of joy and relief at her visit were best kept to myself. Until I could work out what I was going to do long term. Whether we could date or whether I had to devote myself to the business and give up on her. Because Canyon Country Mart left no time for relationships or even going to the bathroom.

Predictably, she asked, "Can I—"

"You don't need to ask." My tone was more brusque than I would have liked, but having her here and knowing I couldn't spend very much time with her was hard. "Hazelnut latte?" I asked, this time friendlier.

She nodded, pulled off the hat her mom knitted, smiled, and went through the back office door to the employees-only bathroom. After making sure Antonio could hold down the fort, I took Sabrina's coffee and one of the coconut cream smoothies that weren't selling out to the store's little porch.

Sabrina came out with the store's dog bowl and filled it for Spencer, who lapped greedily. The dog looked blissed out from the longer hikes she'd been taking while training.

She took the coffee and sucked a long sip. She tipped her head up to catch a ray of sun that made its way through the slats of the porch's pergola roof.

"You make great coffee." She put her cup down, then leaned her chin on her hand. The warmth radiating from her deep brown eyes was more than what was coming from the sun. I wanted to melt into those eyes, kiss her until they were unfocused with lust. Instead, I took a deep breath and tried to remember what she'd said. Right. Coffee.

"Learned in France. This vineyard owner in Scherwiller insisted that I learn as a prelude to any discussion about wine."

"I like this guy already." She smiled in a way that let me know what was next. She wanted to see me again at night, somewhere that may involve a bed and nudity and probably hot, sweaty sex. The mere thought of that had blood rushing down below my waist and worried me that if I stood I'd be indecent. I was trying to work out how I could say yes to that when Antonio banged through the door.

"No Sal," he said.

Just like that, real life came crashing in. Women and dating and hot, sweaty sex took a back seat to the crisis at hand every single time.

"What do you mean, 'no Sal'?"

"He's decided to retire," Antonio continued.

"In the middle of a Friday morning?"

"No, man. His kid says that it's been a long time coming. That he's having more bad days than good."

I threw up my hands in frustration. "They couldn't give us more than five minutes' notice?"

"Don't shoot the messenger." Antonio threw up his own hands and went back in the store after a small group hopped out of one of those "tour of the stars' homes" buses.

"Can I help you? Like last time?" Sabrina offered.

"I'd love your help, but I don't think it'll work."

"Why not?"

"We have nothing. Yesterday's lunch was the end of the current stock. Maybe we have a couple pounds of turkey, and the ham that no one orders anymore."

"You could make, like a basket. I got one for the Hollywood Bowl last summer."

"What would you put in it?" I asked. It was grasping at straws, but I'd take any ideas I could get.

"Don't know. Wine." She shook her head. "It's the middle of the day, so maybe not wine. Cheese, upscale but palatable, like Brie or Gouda or a mild blue cheese. Fruit, which in December means maybe apples, pears, or grapes. Bread of course. Or maybe table water crackers or mini toast. I think I saw those in the store."

"You think it would work?"

"What are hungry people going to do? They might grumble, but if they're on a lunch hour or half hour, are they going to have time to go somewhere else? It's Friday, anyway. People are nicer when they only have a few hours' work left. I'd call it a deconstructed sandwich." Sabrina looked at her watch. "I'm going to go into your mom's office, then I'll come back and help you."

I had to admire her decisiveness. Out of other options, after we walked into the store, I nodded in agreement. She poked around the deli counter before going to my mother's desk and getting to work. I brought Antonio up to speed on the plan, and my employee started gathering supplies.

"Okay, here you go." Sabrina offered up a stack of neat, small squares of paper. Both Antonio and I picked one up. In just a few minutes, she'd managed to make a tiny menu with some kind of flower border and one of those fonts that made everything look that much more upscale. A whole lot different than my mother's love of easy-to-read Arial.

"How..." I trailed off. It was like she'd created a little bit of magic in just a few minutes.

"I did go to design school. Super easy. Now, what are we going to put these deconstructed ingredients in?"

"I have some boxes in the back..."

I led the way through the office to the little storage shed my parents had tacked on to the building.

"No spiders or serial killers are going to jump out, right?"

I titled my head. The makeshift shed did need a coat of paint and its door hinge fixed. It could have been straight out of a horror movie. I added scary shed to my mental list of things I needed to upgrade.

"It's safe. Everything's in a sealed bin. Coyotes and critters would dig through everything otherwise." I worked the key into the unused padlock and jiggled it a few times.

"Do you have labels?"

I searched my mind. "In the bottom desk drawer. Mom usually prints her holiday cards here."

"You find something to box lunch in. I'll be in the office."

Antonio and I were checking through the containers when Sabrina came into the main store area fifteen minutes later. She was cutting through the labels with scissors.

"We put these on the outside of the box after you slot the tab."

"What—"

I picked up the label and my heart nearly stuttered to a stop. She'd done up a proper logo in a few minutes. There was a half-full red wine glass in the middle. The current year was split on both sides of the glass. Under that were the words WINE + GLEN, LUNCH + GLEN, and FOOD + GLEN alternately on different labels. At the bottom, it had "Since 1962," the year my grandparents had started the store.

I snapped my open jaw shut.

"Just a bit of branding. Couldn't decide on the best word combo, so did three different. Which one do you want?"

"Food plus Glen, I think, as we're off Beverly Glen. These are—"

"No big deal," she said, brushing away the compliment I was about to give her. "Let's get the orders and figure out the best way to do this."

Turkey sandwiches were transformed into a box that

held slices of rolled deli meats, Brie, apricot jam, dried fruit, nuts, and mini toast. Ham and roast beef orders were similarly transformed. Tubes of Boursin, wedges of cheddar, all the almonds and pistachios, and the grapes and Valencia oranges, and a lot of crackers. The mini muffins that didn't sell in packs of six were distributed among the boxes. When all was said and done, the three of use alternated dropping in plastic forks and knives. Sabrina found great enjoyment at plopping the FOOD + GLEN stickers on the top of each order.

"You're like a kid," I said. The joy she felt made me feel lighter in the face of what could have been a disaster.

"Who doesn't love stickers?"

"Adult men."

Antonio, who was mostly silent except when talking to customers, barked out a huge laugh at that.

"There are five left. Come sit next to me." She patted the bench behind the deli counter.

I peeled and stuck the first. "Crap," I exclaimed. There was a crease right in the middle of the sticker. She'd made it look so easy.

Her hands went up like a cheerleader's. "All of my years of stickering have finally paid off. You should thank your lucky stars that the winter I was eleven was the worst snow lower B.C. had ever seen. I created a dozen themed sticker albums."

"Themes?" I tried to imagine a coltish young girl studiously pasting stickers in books while snow fell outside. Curiosity about her grew the longer I spent time with her.

Her upbringing had been very different than mine in a lot of ways, more than the obvious different countries, cultures, and me having a movie-star mom.

"One was scratch and sniff. Kind of didn't work out because the smells kind of melded into a toxic brew. But there was one for horses, another for puffy stickers, glitter, and so on."

"I'm happy that you've shared your considerable talents with me."

"Maybe I'll find some puffy glitter stickers for you..." Her smile lit up her face.

"I'm not joking at all, really. What you've done is amazing."

"We'll see. The reception may not be great. People don't like change." Full of bravado an hour ago, she was showing signs of trepidation with her plan.

"It's lunch, not a new car." I nudged her shoulder with mine. The bell over the door started chiming insistently. The clock above the door showed it was quarter to twelve. Time for the lunch rush. "Let's go."

Sabrina, Antonio, and I passed out lunches and handed out orders as efficiently as we could. Sabrina kept a smile on her face the whole time, graciously accepting compliments on the glittering necklace she wore against a chocolate-brown sporty turtleneck that matched her eyes.

We were down to a few lunches when Steve Boyd came into the shop.

Steve was what the word stereotype had been invented for. A successful producer, he had the requisite Porsche, dark-as-night sunglasses, and twenty-year-old assistant who must have been busy with an even more menial task than her usual as lunch gopher.

I moved closer to Sabrina to create a united front against the complaint I was sure was coming.

Steve pushed his glasses up on his waxed hair. I took in a breath, readying myself.

"Hey, man, what's this?" Steve asked.

"Deconstructed roast beef," I explained, doing my best to hide my nerves. Steve's assistant ordered lunch from Canyon Country Mart every day, but seemed to be constantly irritated nonetheless. She claimed that Steve was really picky and the store's fare, more often than not, didn't live up to the producer's standards. More than once, I'd asked my parents why they didn't tell one of Steve's ever-changing assistants that they might find more agreeable food elsewhere, saving everyone the hassle. Steve was the son of a friend, my mom had said, closing the subject.

"Boursin? Blue cheese and walnuts? This is great, man, really great. I hate sandwiches. Always have, but this has been my every assistant's go-to for years and getting any one of them to change is nearly impossible. If you keep this up, I'm totally gonna stop pestering her for sushi."

I tried to hide my confusion. Maybe Sabrina was right and people could handle change.

After that, it was easy handing out the boxes. The rest of the response was overwhelmingly positive. There were a few who didn't think messing with the traditional sandwich was a good idea, but everyone else was thrilled.

"That went well," Sabrina said. Her face dimpled into a full-fledged smile, her second today. The arms that wound around my neck and the kiss that was planted on my lips was spontaneous and oh so good. I wanted to kick out Antonio, lock the door, and finish what they were apparently starting. Like a good store manager, though, I removed my tongue and stepped back a couple of paces.

"I need to get the lunch stuff cleaned up."

Rejection flitted across her face before her usual half smile replaced it. "I'll help before I get back to my own work."

"Any progress on the mystery of the platinum?" She was so good at problem solving, I hoped she'd been able to apply it to her own and not just mine.

"Not really." She shook her head, smile disappearing into a pensive frown. "Let's not talk about that. This, at least, was a win."

Antonio was going back and forth between the walk-in, storing unused items. I was ringing up a steady line of customers at the register, and Sabrina was cleaning the knives and slicers. It reminded me that often working in the store wasn't all bad. There were times like this when it was a companionable group endeavor that gave everyone satisfaction from hard work done.

"You don't have to do that, you know."

"It's fine. Hard labor never killed anyone. I like feeling useful..." She turned back to the cheese slicer for only a second before I heard her yelp in pain. "Ow. God. Oh, shit."

I whipped my head around. I'd never heard Sabrina curse, even when she was watching the Critics' Choice Awards and that actress's necklace had fallen apart.

"What's wrong?"

"Cut my finger."

"I'll get a bandage," Antonio volunteered before disappearing in the office.

Sabrina came from behind the sneeze guard and sat on the floor between the deli counter and the cash register.

"Do you have paper towels? Not the bathroom kind, but the super absorbent kind. You know, from the commercial where they pick up a puppy or baby with a wet one."

Lead replaced the low-grade lust that had been humming through me all morning. There was a lot of blood. I could see the finger, though, so that was still intact.

"Jesus. There's blood on your arm," I said. She was holding up her finger and applying lots of pressure, but the bleeding didn't look like it was slowing. With every beat of her heart, more spilled.

"I'm so sorry." She pressed harder, her fingers going white. "This is such a mess. I'll clean it up. Don't worry, I'm an expert at blood removal."

I wasn't worried about the wood floor. God knew all it had seen in the last fifty-plus years; it was her health I was worried about far more. "Wait, is this because of the heart surgery? You said something about blood thinners." My heart sped up. I took a deep breath so that I didn't add my own cardiac event to what was happening in front of me. "I'll call nine-one-one."

"I don't need an ambulance. Paper towels, though, that could help."

"Right. Okay." I tripped over the rubber mat behind the counter in my hurry to find them. Then my hand hit the counter before I righted myself. For a split second, I wondered if it would bruise, and could something as simple as that kill her. Shaking off the thought, I went and found the towels and handed a large wad to Sabrina.

"I can't find the first-aid kit," Antonio reported after he emerged from the back.

I thought back to the last store inspection. The county had deducted points for the missing kit. It hadn't been replaced. Another one for my never-ending list.

"Do we need to call someone?" I asked Sabrina, worried that the absent kit would be the difference between life and death.

"Calm down. I'm not going to die on your store's floor. Get my backpack."

"What's in it?" I asked, while the debate between calling nine-one-one and getting the pack raged in my head.

"I'm bleeding here. Can you just get it, please?"

"Sorry." I ran to the office and pulled her leather pack off the office chair.

"Can you unzip it? There's a pouch in there that says 'homeostatic gauze.' Please open it and get the gauze out."

I followed her instructions to the letter, finding the packet and pulling it from the bag. "Now what?"

"Open it. Pull out the gauze. Wrap it around my finger."

"Right. Okay..."

"It'll stop bleeding in a second." She dropped her voice to a whisper. "Go help that guy who's wandering up and down the wine aisle. Everything about him says he has a date, the very significant third one. A cooking dinner date, and he's nervous about what to do. Gotta help him because I want him to have great sex. Everybody deserves that."

Not sure whether to laugh or worry, I levered myself up and sent up silent thanks that the magic gauze seemed to be working. As soon as the customer left, I'd make that next date, if only to convince her the Kilimanjaro climb was the worst idea ever for someone with her condition. I really liked her and very much wanted her to live well past the spring.

Chapter Eleven

SABRINA

"ARE YOU IN HIBERNATION OR SOMETHING?"
Mona's body was in an aggressive stance that had challenge written all over it.

I had let Mona through the front door and up into my
studio. From my friend's question, it was starting to feel
like the day's first mistake was opening that door. Sure to
be one of many. After all, with the self-destructing jewelry
and Henry-related mishaps, I was on a bit of a roll.

"More like exile."

I didn't want to have Henry look at me like I was going
to die or my other friends over only to have them give me
those pitying smiles. I looked from my workbench toward
the armchair that Mona had curled into, boots and all.

"Do people still do that, exile?"

"You mean leave the country where they committed a
crime to take up residence in London or Madrid?" Mona
asked.

"And France, don't forget Paris. Deposed dictators love the French capital. No one ever goes into exile in Saskatchewan or New Jersey."

"You know logic dictates that for you to go into exile, you'd have to move to a new country, 'cause you're not in your home country."

"L.A. is exile already, then?"

I dropped my pliers in frustration. Despite beating my head against the metaphorical wall, I wasn't any closer to figuring out how I was going to fix my jewelry designs. Today, I was working on a simple commission—a wedding set.

Something foolproof.

"Maybe it's just hell on earth," I concluded grumpily. I looked at the clock hung near the pitched ceiling beams. There was still time to crawl back into bed, maybe try getting out another day.

"Whoa there. You've got a roof over your head, food in your fridge, and your health. So hell isn't the word I'd use," Mona rebuked. Softening her expression, she said, "Is this about the jewelry or the guy?"

I thought about my friend's question for a really long time.

"Henry's really cool, I guess. He's a little freaked out about the climb and stuff, but cool."

"So are you guys going out? Is that why he's worried about doing the really, really long-distance thing?"

Why did everyone around me treat climbing Kilimanjaro like I was taking a six-month sabbatical in a place with no post, phone, or internet?

"We're not in grade nine. I like him. We've had a good time together."

I wasn't ready to admit to myself that it was something more than a good time, much less to Mona, queen of the two-date relationship.

"But we both have a lot going on. He's got the store to manage now, and I've got to get my head wrapped around the jewelry I have yet to construct for the Golden Globes and Oscars."

"Do you think the cameo is an omen?" Mona's question was such a non sequitur that it took me a long second to respond.

Finally, I said, "Now you're the one talking in mazes and riddles."

"Like some outside force is telling you that you need to go for it?"

I ran downstairs and fished through the bowl on the entrance table by her door. Through paper clips and loose change, I found it. Came back up. Handed it to Mona.

Free of the cursed thing, I sat back on the bench. "What about it?"

Mona's silver stacking rings gleamed in the sunlight as she fingered the jet.

"I think it wants you to find love."

"Oh my God, please, not with the mystical. I thought I was crazy. Now I'm thinking we might need adjoining suites on the psych ward."

"Just saying. It's got a corny love poem. You met a guy that you're holding at arm's length. Maybe you should just give in to it."

"Henry? Jeez, I've got way more pressing stuff to deal with."

"Henry. Because at the end of the day, the stones and celebrities aren't going to love you, but Henry might."

I pretended to pick up something from the floor. I had no poker face and didn't want my friend to know that somewhere deep, I wished for that. Maybe in a few years, it would be the perfect time once my career was on cruise control. Not now, though. Not now when everything was just beginning to pop and there was hope that this may be the year my career took off. The year I hiked a mountain and figured out who I really was other than the girl with the heart condition.

"We've gone on like two dates." I hoped that I'd convincingly minimized the relationship between myself and Henry. "That...does not make for love."

Mona shook her head like she'd suddenly developed a belief in love at first sight.

"Do you like him at least?"

"Sure. A lot. He's as great a guy, maybe even better than I imagined. But um, job, and the climb, and living my life."

"Just saying."

"I appreciate your advice, but I've got to get these stones set." With tweezers, I counted out the eighteen white sapphires that would decorate the twist around the main stone. Next, I lined up the nearly three-carat cushion-cut sapphire. That would go last.

In a grand imitation of Spencer, Mona walked the perimeter, lifting and setting down various portfolio pieces I kept on hand when customers needed to see in-person samples.

A low bark came from Spencer, then high-pitched whining. Both my hands were occupied setting the first of the small sapphires. "Can you answer that?"

"Answer what?" Mona asked, seconds before the doorbell rang.

"Seriously? You can tell the bell is going to ring before it does? You're creeping me out."

"Seriously. I have a dog. You figure them out pretty quick."

Mona's eyebrows were nearly lost under sharply cut jet-black bangs.

"I'll play. What did Spencer tell you?"

"That someone's at the door. It's not the mailman or a package delivery guy. And Spencer knows who it is."

Mona tossed me a look that practically yelled crazy-pants as she thumped down the stairs in heavy boots. Two different pairs of shoes thumped back up the wood stairs. I figured it was one of our neighbors appealing in person about a block watch or the city's garbage service. There had certainly been a lot of those kinds of e-mails flying around on the neighborhood app.

"Look what the cat...no...dog dragged in."

I finished bending the last prong on the stone I was setting before I looked up.

Henry.

Without a moment's hesitation, he came across the room and kissed me full on the mouth.

If I hadn't had a death grip on the pliers, they'd have fallen from my hand for the second time that afternoon. I returned his kiss, probably rubbing my lips against his a beat too long. The contact, no matter how brief, was so good I didn't want to stop.

The click, click, clicking of my valve was the only sound I could hear. It was so loud I was sure it was echoing off the walls. Thank goodness my friends were too polite to mention the sound or the obvious reason for it.

"So that's *my* cue," Mona announced, looking like she was about to head out.

"You don't have to go," I replied automatically. I had never been the kind of girl, nor did I want to be the kind of woman, who tossed my friends on their ear the minute a man walked into my life, much less the room.

"I came to check that everything's okay with your hand," Henry said, squatting down next to my work bench. Gently, he loosened my death grip on my tools and took my hands in his. I hoped the tremors that shook my body weren't visible to anyone. I was still first-date nervous around him despite us doing the deed.

"It's fine." I tried to pull my hands away from him, but he kept a gentle grip.

"What happened?" Mona asked, her voice full of concern.

Here we go. This was why I kept my condition and subsequent surgery a secret.

"Cut myself helping out with Henry's lunch rush. No big deal." My attempt at being casual had failed miserably. It was too quick, my explanation. Mine were the kind of rushed words that left nothing but questions. I snatched my hand back from Henry. Picked up the pliers again as if I were going to get something more done. But my nerves were shot. Shaky hands and custom jewelry creation did not go hand in hand.

"It's a huge deal, Sabrina. A huge...frickin'...deal. If I'd known that a simple cut would do that to you, I wouldn't have let you help in the store." He said it with all the sincerity in the world. But I didn't want my condition to hobble me.

"That's just it, Henry. It was lunch, not tree trimming with an unguarded chainsaw. This...*this* is why I don't tell people."

"Tell people what?" Mona asked. Her head, ink-black fringe moving in tempo, swiveled between me and Henry.

"Oh, I didn't realize..." Henry trailed off.

"That I have an artificial heart valve." I spit it out plain and simple, like I'd been asked my name, rank, and serial number.

"What does that mean?" Mona's usual delivery was strictly deadpan, so the concern in her voice was disconcerting.

"I have a piece of titanium in my chest that keeps me from dying. But in order for my body to not reject the transplant, I have to take medication daily. That same medication makes it so I don't clot. I get cut, I bleed until I can stop the flow or I have to go to the hospital. That's it in a nutshell. Questions?"

Unexpectedly, Mona's voice went up yet another octave. "I had no idea. If I'd known, I would—"

"—have treated me differently. I don't want people to treat me like I'm some fragile sixteenth-century Ming vase."

"You could have told me. I would have figured it out." And Mona was probably right. My friend *would* have figured it out—how to be okay with my heart. Mona was a virtual paragon of adaptability and acceptance. I don't know where she'd grown those genes, or if it was an L.A. thing, but it made me love her all the more for it.

"You know now. But that doesn't mean that I can't help you load your pieces into vans, or can't help you cut veg in your kitchen. Okay?"

My friend gathered me in an uncharacteristically swift hug. "Gotcha back," she whispered. "Gotta go, though. Three's a crowd," she said loud enough for Henry to hear. "Don't need a front-row seat to a clone of the Grissoms."

Heat came to my face, fast and blazing hot. I stammered out, "I thought we were going to—"

At the door to the room, Mona pounded her chest twice with her fist then threw out the peace sign. A minute later, I heard the front door close.

"The Grissoms?" he asked.

A knot of embarrassment and desire sat low in my stomach.

"Neighbors."

"How would we be cloning them?"

Only under pain of death would I answer that one.

"So I'm almost one hundred percent."

Blood didn't seem like such a bad topic. In supplication, I held up my hand and removed my work gloves. A simple bandage covered the wound. "Fine. I'm fine. It was just a nick. Working today with no problem."

Henry's eyes widened. I wanted to tell him that he'd be crap at poker and that no I wasn't on the verge of death every time I cut myself.

"I came for another reason." With his graceful avoidance of anything more on the topic of the neighbors or clotting gauze, he could be an honorary Canadian. None of that in-your-face American stuff from him today.

I pointed to the small wrapped package in his hand. "Is that the reason?"

A huge smile broke out on his face. I smiled back. His joy *was* infectious. "Christmas present."

Panic made my heart trip and the valve click. Right. It was December. We were sleeping together, if not dating, so of course some kind of present exchange should happen. "Should" being the operative word. I'd gotten my parents gifts before the shopping rush and hadn't had a thought about going back out to battle mall traffic to get something for Henry.

Not a day without a faux pas. If things didn't change soon, it would be my motto.

"Uh," tripped from my lips.

His smile widened. "I'm not expecting reciprocation." He'd read me like a book. "It's a gift. Open it."

Pulling the utility knife from the canister in front of me, I slipped it slowly under the tape, careful not to tear the gold and black paper. I opened the small box to reveal two tickets from the Academy of Motion Picture Arts and Sciences. I had to squint to read them. They weren't glossy or over the top like I'd have thought.

"Wow. Thanks so much." I stood and threw my arms around his neck. My kisses landed high on both his cheeks. Henry colored a bit. "This is so cool," I said. "I've never been to the Oscars." The thought of seeing Hollywood royalty in person almost overrode the trepidation I felt about not being safely miles from what could be my next metallurgic disaster.

"I promised we could see your jewelry in person."

"Right. Yeah." The reason behind the tickets sucked the euphoria from my excitement. The commissions hadn't been canceled, but I wouldn't be surprised to find out that my clients were making alternative arrangements. At least I could enjoy the spectacle of the show and hope that next year was better.

"Have you gotten any closer to figuring it out?" Henry asked.

Sitting back at the bench, I pulled a length of wire from a large wood spool and began working with it. I unwound the metal, snipped it with one tool, then began twisting with another.

"I e-mailed a bunch of metallurgical experts I know, but it's the holidays."

"Speaking of... What are you doing for Christmas?"

"I'm supposed to be at home. In Vancouver," I clarified. "Mom's probably got a new handmade sweater for me under the tree."

"But you canceled that. So are you doing something with Mona?"

I glanced toward the necklace perched on a wood form on my bench. "Kind of under deadline here. I braved the long lines and sent my gifts on by post. Mom will be disappointed that I'm not getting on a last-minute flight, but—"

"Come to my house."

"What?" I wondered if I'd heard him right.

"We can put up a tree. I'll make something. Come on, it'll be fun. Tomorrow's Christmas Eve. No one should be alone on Christmas Eve."

"Can I bring Spencer? I mean, I wouldn't ask..." I trailed off immediately, wishing I *hadn't* asked. Dinner wasn't an overnight invitation. Because obviously I could leave my adult dog home for a few hours, but overnight was tough. I didn't want Spencer to have to hold it in any longer than necessary. Of course, I'd spoken too soon. Mona could have let the dog out.

I closed my eyes for a brief moment. Would there ever be a time when things weren't awkward between us?

"You know it's okay. It's great having a dog around after Sadie..."

Great.

He was thinking about euthanasia and I was thinking about sex. One day this had to get easier. The whole dating, girl-guy thing. Suddenly, I wished I'd had more practice before Henry. That I hadn't been so self-conscious about the long scar in the middle of my chest. Maybe then, I'd have been ready for him. Because I so much wanted to be ready. Perhaps I could clear my head in Tanzania, learn bravery and courage. Come back a new and improved woman strong enough for a real relationship.

Henry sat on the plush armchair I considered my thinking spot, the place where I sat when I needed inspiration or to work out a problem. I'd been sitting there quite a bit over the last weeks.

"This is not purple." He smoothed his hands along the rolled arms.

"Too much of a good thing and all that." It was a very conservative navy canvas with white piping. I watched Henry struggle with the throw pillow before standing, lifting it from the chair, sitting, and putting it in his lap.

"Would you all...men, I mean...just live with a single black leather couch and a big-screen TV?"

Henry's half smile gave me a clue as to how his place was probably furnished, though for him, I'd guess the couch was brown.

"Your house is nice, really comfortable. But if I had to be an interior decorator, I'd totally fail." Holding the throw pillow aloft, he said, "Where do you even buy all this stuff?"

"They have stores full of accessories everywhere. Especially West Hollywood. What streets were you looking at for your wine shop?"

The slight wince in his eyes made my own gut twist a bit. His parents' last-minute South Seas vacation had most certainly put the kibosh on that. He hadn't mentioned it more than that one time. Everything was a minefield with that topic, so I'd stayed away.

"Melrose. Near San Vicente," he gamely answered.

"Half your customers would probably have come from the Pacific Design Center. That's all accessories..."

I turned back to the jewelry in front of me. Pliers in hand, I placed a stone, bent prongs, and examined my work. Lifting the loupe to my eye, I examined the piece for any sharp edges that would catch on a dress or rub at someone's finger.

"That's cute that you actually use that. It's like a jewelry heist movie with the jeweler in the back, checking out the diamonds. What are you looking for anyway?"

"Come over here," I said, my motives anything but pure. I wanted to close the distance between us. Talk of loupes and pillows was okay, but I wanted to breathe in the scent of him. Distract him with kisses that would lead to something far more pleasurable than manipulating metal.

I handed him the magnifying lens. "What do you see?"

He leaned in, pressing his eye to the glass.

"These stones are amazing," Henry said. "Up close you

can see why people like bling so much. Wow." He backed up a bit, his warmth no longer near. "Looks perfect. Have you figured out the...uh...problem?" His eyes were turned to the half-finished pieces perched high on the shelf atop my bench.

Dread pushed out the pleasant feeling of my insides filling with butterflies. That nervous feeling that was only cured with kissing faded as reality crept in.

Other than Henry, it was the only thing I could think about. I shared my half-baked theory with him.

"I've been using more and heavier stones than I ever have. Maybe it's a flaw in design, needing a heavier gauge wire or something. Don't know. I've been racking my brain for days. I have to deliver my next piece in a couple of weeks."

He leaned in closer, peered at the unfinished pieces. "And your necklaces are silver?"

"Silver tarnishes. Yellow gold isn't popular anymore, except maybe for disaster planning. These are platinum."

I was looking at his lips, imagining all the things they could do, had done to me, when I should have been paying attention to my work. I'd removed my gloves when I'd been showing Henry first my hands, then the loupe, so the prong I'd been bending in place slipped from the tool's grip and cut deep into the middle finger of my left hand.

"Crap!" I dropped the necklace and the tools to the desk and immediately pulled at the top right drawer of my work bench.

"What's up?"

"Pricked my finger. Gimme a sec." Like I'd done the other day, I pulled out a strip of the medicated gauze and held it to my finger. It was a smallish cut in circumference that stopped bleeding almost immediately. I tried to keep my sigh of relief to myself. Clotting disorders were not sexy. Fortunately, this cut hadn't been life threatening.

"All fixed," I chirped as I applied one of the thousands of bandages I kept around the house for just such instances.

I stood and stretched. Like a teenager with no game. I took our proximity as an opportunity to lay a hand against the flannel covering his chest. When the look of concern didn't clear from his eyes, I stood on my tiptoes and brought his lips to mine. Before they closed, his blue eyes had glazed over with want, need, desire, the worry in them gone.

This.

This is what we did best. I walked him backward until he fell back into the empty chair. He held out his arms and I sat across his lap. With Henry captive, I was able to explore him like I hadn't been able to the last time, when he'd called the shots and had gotten me so riled up I hadn't been able to think straight.

Not shying away from his gaze, I met it head-on. Then I ran shaky fingers through his hair. Its autumn-leaf-at-fall color was so amazing, I was almost jealous. I followed his sideburns to his close-cropped beard. Facial hair was sexy as hell on him. I kissed him high on his cheeks, then near the corner of his mouth, the friction delicious.

"Were you ever clean-shaven?" I'd absentmindedly wondered what it would be like to have his clean-shaven skin rub across my belly, in between my parted thighs.

"Maybe a few years back. I grew the hair when I was traveling. Easier to maintain if there's a day when I can't get a shave in."

Winding my hands around his neck, I kissed him full on the mouth. He didn't hesitate a moment before he was opening and exploring me with his hot, silky tongue. Compelled to share the feelings that were overwhelming me, I pulled back a hairsbreadth.

"I missed you."

"You were at the store yesterday."

"Let me be more specific." I brought my lips to his ear, nibbled on the lobe, then whispered, "I missed this."

Sticking my finger through each fabric hole, I released first one button, then the rest of his shirt. I spread the soft flannel aside and scraped my fingernails against the ribbing of the fitted tank underneath. I could feel the beat of his heart through my fingers. An answering pulse between my legs thrummed deep.

Henry's capable hands made short work of the ties on my navy peasant blouse. One minute I was following the line of his collarbone to the divot between before making my way down the hard contour of his pecs, then the next minute, air coursed against my belly as the blouse billowed above my head and floated to the floor like a feather.

It took all my willpower to not cross my arms. Instead, I gathered up the confidence I'd developed over the last weeks and leaned into Henry. His arms banded around my back. I sank into his warmth, then met his lips again. We kissed for a long moment. My breasts pushed against the bra and camisole. For the first time in a decade, I wondered why in the hell I had on so many clothes.

"What's that upstairs?" Henry's breath against my neck caused me to shiver.

"My John Malkovich room." His head cocked in question. I stood and whipped off the high-necked camisole. "You should come up. Duck your head."

Lured by the prospect of my nudity, I hoped, he followed me upstairs, keeping his head down. I sat on one of four five-by-five-foot pillows my mom had stitched for me after seeing the room. Sitting on the floor minimized the chances of bumping my head. Following my example, he did the same.

"Purple again?"

"Mom again."

"It was you this time. Wasn't me who brought up a mom." He threw his hands in the air. His blank tank lifted. The rich auburn hair arrowed down to the gleaming buckle that held up his dark jeans. An index finger unhooked the buckle and released the prong. The snap and zipper posed no resistance to my hands. Levering myself back up, I kissed his lips, but pulled away before I lost control. The shirt had to go. A few seconds later, I made that happen. Then I coaxed him to lift his hips.

"I love that you wear boxers."

"I hear they're not hip."

"You don't have to be hip." He was hot enough to wear almost anything and make it look like the latest fashion. I placed a kiss on one hip bone. Pulled down the shorts a bit more and kissed the other one. One swift tug and they were off. In his birthday best, he was magnificent. All hard and pulsing, fluid weeping from the tip. I wanted nothing more than to envelop him in my mouth, bring him half the pleasure he'd brought me last week.

"Not this time."

"It's not...it's not for the same reason...as before." This time it wasn't about hiding. Instead it was about exploring the boundaries of his pleasure.

"Oh, honey. I want that. You have no idea how much. But I want other things too."

"Like what?"

"Like this."

He turned the tables. One minute I was leaning over him, then the next, I was supine on the screen-printed fabric.

"The bra's going to have to go. The same for the pants. They're cute, but not as cute as you."

I wanted to be modest. I wanted to care about my scar, my inexperience, but I didn't give a toss about any of it during this heated moment. All I wanted was to make Henry feel good, to have Henry make *me* feel good.

He kissed me then, an all-consuming kiss that singed me all the way to my lilac toenails. Henry palmed my cheek, then skimmed down my side. He made a stop at my breast. My sudden intake of breath had him lifting his head and hand.

"You okay?"

"More than okay." I took his hand and placed it back on my bared breast. Even though I knew it was coming, the contact sent an electric current directly between my legs. I squeezed them together, trying to keep the pleasure from brimming over so quickly.

Henry rubbed a thumb back and forth across my nipple. I couldn't help the moan that escaped my lips. God, he could bring me to the brink with a single touch. I undulated my hips. Henry's other hand was on me in an instant. My stomach quivered when he brushed past my belly button to the warm place between my thighs. Two strong fingers separated my folds, while the middle finger landed on my clit.

For a second I seriously worried that I'd hit the sloped roof. But when I opened my eyes, both Henry and I were still on solid ground. With his free arm, he gathered me close to him. His heat warmed me as much as what he was doing. Spontaneous combustion was becoming a reality. I hoped my propane torches were safe.

"Damn, Sabrina. You're like all my fantasies come true," he said before he dropped his head to my breast. His lips closed on a nipple at the same time his finger increased its friction on my clit.

"I want you inside me," I said.

"I want you to come first."

"That's not fair," I gasped.

"Oh, honey. That's more than fair."

I didn't have the breath to argue. It took all my concentration just to breathe, keep my toes from curling hard enough to cramp my muscles. His biceps flexed and brought me even closer. He left my most private area bereft for a moment as he lifted my leg over his, giving him even greater access. He took advantage, notching his rock-hard cock where his fingers had been. He titled my chin up a bit and my eyes opened. His own were as blue as the sky at dusk, as intense as lasers. I wanted to look away, but his miniscule shake of the head kept my focus on him.

I didn't break our stare as his cock did magical things to me.

"Oh...oh!" It was a total surprise when I came. One minute we were locking eyes, and in the next it was as if tiny summertime sparklers were going off everywhere in my body. When I opened my eyes again, Henry was still there. Though his eyes weren't as clear as before. I broke eye contact to look between them. The hand that had been gripping my hip had a tight-fisted hold on his own cock. It was sheathed in a condom and pulsing slightly.

He slipped and notched at my opening.

"Is this okay?"

"God, yes. Now. Please," I whimpered.

One second I was begging and in the next, I was filled to the hilt.

"Look at me."

I did what he asked and my pussy clenched.

"Yes, Sabrina. Yes. Do that again."

This time I intentionally focused on my Kegel muscles, squeezing when he was in deep.

"I can't hold out much longer."

"You don't have to."

His right hand left my hip and came up to my hair, combing the long strands, then made its way to my breast. He plumped and squeezed. Flicking his finger over my taut nipple made me stutter in the steady beat of his thrusts. Together we watched my nipple get pinker and harder. With one deep thrust and a hoarse shout, he found fulfillment. I too felt tiny pulses inside. Though not as intense as the last, my second orgasm was still good.

Henry pulled out and lay on his back. I followed suit and the room came back into focus as our breathing deepened. I reached out my hand and dragged a crochet afghan over us both. Without pleasure coursing through my veins, my other problems came back into sharp focus.

Sex was a fun distraction. But it was still only that—a distraction.

Flipping onto my belly, I traced the hairs on his chest. They were springy and surprisingly soft.

"I really need to figure this damned thing out."

"Kind of like the wine and vinegar problem..."

I didn't hear anything else Henry said because I was thinking about tarnish on silver. Platinum didn't tarnish, but it had its own Achilles' heel. It wasn't oxygen or sulfides that wrecked this metal, it was carbon. The first lesson of platinum working was a spotless environment. I'd learned that years ago when I'd taken advanced metal-smithing.

Throwing back the afghan, careful of my head, I stood and ran down the steps and into my studio. I picked up my gloves from the bench and slipped them on. With a loupe in hand, I looked at the pieces I was working on for the two remaining awards shows.

Just as I'd thought—brown specks.

"Can I see your etchings?" His half smile was contagious. The unmitigated disaster that was my career didn't seem so dire with Hottie McHotHot leaning against the newel post. He'd gone to the bathroom and climbed up to the loft and come back down with boxers and his tank, my blouse in hand.

"You can look but not touch."

"Since when is touching a problem?" He handed me the shirt. I slipped it over my body before we got distracted with round two.

I could feel my face heat with the double entendre. Purple toenails and a lot of bare leg were exposed as I straddled my work bench in only my peasant blouse and the underwear I'd picked up along the way.

"Outside of this room, it's not. You know how you said some weird bacteria could turn wine to vinegar?"

He nodded.

"Well, carbon can turn platinum into breakaway jewelry."

"How do you avoid contamination?"

"By keeping my gloves on at all times. Using solvents to clean it if my finger does get pricked."

"Do you get hurt that often?"

"No more than the average jewelry maker. Sharp stones, metal burrs. I can usually stop it, but with these fiddly designs, I've probably hurt myself more than usual."

I looked at him for signs of freaking out, but he looked pretty stable. Maybe people could get over it, not be shocked by it all, not freaked out by my cutting veg or hiking mountains.

"You think you can fix it?"

With newfound confidence, I answered, "Most definitely. Now only if I can win back everyone's trust at the same time."

Chapter Twelve

HENRY

THE DOORBELL PEALED through rooms of my parents' house. A stripped-down version of Beethoven's Fifth symphony echoed off the clean white walls.

Shearling jacket buttoned up tight to her neck, Sabrina stood on the tiny tiled entrance area, only a single step up from the curb. I opened the carved Moroccan double gate and let her and the dog through.

"You can take him off leash," I offered. "The yard's fenced. Coyotes can't get up and over from the hillside."

"Great." Sabrina unhooked the dog, who was happy to go exploring, then hefted a large leather tote higher on her shoulder.

I closed and locked the wooden gate behind her.

"You didn't need to bring anything," I started. "I've got dinner covered."

She hesitated, then paused. I turned to see her face turn red and blotchy with what I thought may be embarrassment. She did that a lot...blushed. It was so damned adorable, I wanted to make it happen again and again. I watched her stammer out an explanation.

"I...uh...brought a change of clothes. You know, in case I need to...um...change."

Change? I grasped for something to say to put her at ease, all the while figuring out why she'd want to change her clothes.

"Pine sap can be a bear to get out," I offered.

"So this...this is Casa Barnhill?" She stuttered out her question, sounding first-date nervous. We were beyond that, though. I'd been to her house. Made friends with her dog, who was at this moment sniffing and peeing his way along the perimeter fence. Made love with her. I shook my head, reminding myself that everything didn't need to be figured out. I turned to Sabrina pointing out my parents' house on one side, my guest house on the other, and the pool and hot tub that divided the two.

As we crossed the last patch of lawn to come to the huge French doors that served as an entryway, I got it.

She thought she was staying overnight, because you didn't invite a girl for dinner, and tree trimming, and drinking, and maybe even sex, if she had to do the walk—or drive —of shame in the wee hours of the morning.

It was too damn late to say anything now. I expelled a breath, vowing to work on my communication, because it was becoming increasingly important that Sabrina understand my feelings for her, what those feelings were becoming.

"Let me give you the ten-cent tour." I took the leather satchel from her shoulder and laid it on the piano bench, trying not to imagine what kind of pajamas a woman brought when she planned to spend the night with a man.

I showed her the neat bedrooms and bathrooms that no one was using. Her eyebrows shot up at the small screening room that replaced what had probably originally been a family room.

"What's that smell?" she asked upon entering the kitchen.

"Red wine hot chocolate. I figured we'd have a little while we were setting up the tree."

"But you live in that other house?"

I pointed out of the floor-to-ceiling windows of the living room. "Right over there. There's storage underneath and my place is up those stairs." We'd go there later, most definitely because sex in my parents' house squicked me out. I'd never done it in here even when I'd been a teenager and had nowhere to go. My brother, Evan, had claimed the guest house first. The minute he'd gone to college, though, I had staked it out. Brought my high school dates there just outside the watchful eyes of Mom and Dad.

"Is that Jill Mathis?" Sabrina pointed at the wall-size mural painted on the side of the pool house. It was an ode to my mother. Back in her heyday, some suitor had done it to win her over. Hadn't worked. My dad had won hands down. But the picture, some one-of-a-kind masterpiece, to hear my mom tell it, stayed. "Your hair totally reminds me of hers."

Sabrina might speak English, with nearly zero accent, but I was reminded that she was a foreigner not only to America, but to Los Angeles and its celebrity-obsessed culture. Ninety-nine percent of people I met knew full well who I was before I'd even shaken their hands or unnecessarily introduced myself.

"Jill Mathis is my mom."

"Your mom?"

That blush spread again. I guessed Mona hadn't warned her. Nor had Antonio mentioned it. I hated gossip, but half-wished someone else had told her. I could see it working in her mind as she melded her previous knowledge of me with this new revelation.

"Jill Mathis was in all these movies my mom loved. She played Kimberly Welch's mom in a movie. She's been nominated for like three different Academy Awards."

A look of dawning recognition took over her face. She cupped her forehead.

"That's why you have Oscar tickets."

"Nominees become Academy members."

"She stopped acting. My mom always wondered about that." Before I could open my mouth to explain my mother's decision to cut short her career when she had been at the pinnacle of Hollywood popularity, Sabrina waved away any explanation. "My God. I'm not prying. I was just surprised is all. My mom...forget it. Anyway, that's a shock. I mean, I thought you lived with your mom. Now I know that you lived with YOUR MOM." She spoke as if my mom's name was the kind of thing only spoken of in capital letters.

"She changed her last name to Barnhill when she quit."

"What's for dinner?" She wasn't much good at changing the subject, but I gave her a pass. I knew from experience with people outside of Los Angeles that my mom's identity was an odd bit of information for a person to integrate. It was like make-believe suddenly became reality. That integration had happened for me many, many years ago when I first saw my mom on TV pretending to be someone completely different.

"Braised short ribs, buttermilk mashed potatoes, garlic-sautéed kale."

"That sounds amazing. Um...is it in your kitchen over there?" She surreptitiously sniffed around.

"Oh...no. Delivery. I can do a lot, but whip up a meal when the stores are picked clean? Not so much. You know what? Let me turn on the oven. I'll heat it up, if you'll be ready to eat in half an hour."

Sabrina nodded. She took a seat on one of the wrought iron stools and swung her legs back and forth, swiveling the chair.

"Where's the tree?"

"Delivery."

"Is there anything you can't have delivered in L.A.?"

"Not that I know of." My mom had shared tales of nearly everything legal, illicit, and otherwise being driven to the homes of Hollywood's top actors.

"Is that the tree?" Sabrina asked when Beethoven's Fifth struck again.

"Yep. Let's go see what they've got."

We both walked to the front gates this time.

"You've got a tree for us?" I asked the driver decked out in a dark green polo and blinking Santa hat.

"You're at the end of the delivery route. Have a look at what we got left."

I put my foot on the step and swung up into the cargo area. There were exactly two trees left. A pathetic Charlie Brown specimen, and one nearly the length of the truck.

"Tall or short?" I asked Sabrina, resigned to the choices. For all my bravado about delivery, I was pretty sure trees were in short supply on Christmas Eve.

"Tall. I guess. Will that fit in your house?"

"We're about to find out."

The delivery driver gamely dragged the tree, bound in mesh, through the yard to the living room. I threw down the skirt thing that kept the floor from getting scratched and then dragged over the tree holder.

The driver whipped out a pocket knife and slit the mesh. He rolled the tree and balled up the thin plastic.

All three of us lifted and tried to put it in the stand.

"Nope. The tree is a foot taller than the ceiling—at least."

"Already took off the mesh. This one's yours."

Resigned to having not a single thing go right with Sabrina, I followed the guy out, peeled seven twenties from my wallet and handed them to the driver.

When I came back, Sabrina was smiling from ear to ear. I ran to the oven and pulled the food to safety. It had probably been in about ten minutes too long. I peeled back the foil lid. No steam billowed. Not a single stream. I poked my finger into the foil tin. Ice-cold potatoes met my finger. I'd thought I'd turned the oven on. I was almost sure that had been my plan, but once again, the pretty girl had distracted me.

Speaking of pretty girls...

"Why are you smiling?" Her face was split ear to ear like a kid who'd woken up to a living room chock-full of presents on Christmas Day, and not one who was stuck with an ill-sized tree.

"I have the best idea for the too-tall Christmas tree."

"What do you need?" I asked. I was more than happy to leave it to the artist and her vision.

"Pruning shears. A bit of wire."

I thought for a minute. "We'll have to go to the store after dinner. That kind of stuff is there in the shed."

"Let's do it now." She jumped up, and in a second she was back in the brown leather jacket. "The food's in no danger of burning, is it?"

"Nope. Absolutely no danger of that."

Ten minutes later, I pulled my truck into the gravel lot.

With my key in the store's lock, Sabrina holding the screen door away from my back, my earlier happiness at having a pretty girl in my house evaporated. I pushed the door in, the weight of obligation landing on my shoulders.

Without having to look, I flipped four switches. The fluorescent lights hummed to life.

"Oooh. This is cool. I don't think I've ever been in a store when there weren't any shoppers."

"It's not all it's cracked up to be. There should be some wire in the aisle next to the scissors. I'll check the shed."

Sabrina didn't walk down that aisle. Instead, she walked over to the section with wine, then over to the refrigerator case, peering at various items.

"You can pick up anything you want. No cost. Just let me know and I'll make a note."

She didn't pick up a single item though. Her features were screwed up in what I was coming to recognize as her thoughtful face.

"What's the deal with your wine store?" She poked at one shelf then another like a county inspector looking for roaches.

"There is no deal. I can't open it now. No way I can run two businesses. Maybe in a year or two, when I find a few steady employees that don't cost more than the profit margin. My parents operated this place with mostly free labor."

"What was going to be in your wine store?"

"Good lighting, first of all," I said, looking at the greenish tinge the fluorescent bulbs cast.

"Okay, what else?"

"Custom display shelves with insets for boutique wines. Properly calibrated refrigerator display cases with immediately drinkable wines. A small gourmet section like the kind you find in Paris. Charcuterie. Fine cheeses. Imported crackers. That sort of thing." I'd tried to sound offhand, but that was difficult when I could imagine it right down to the rolling tasting island with marble top.

"Sounds really cool. I'd totally shop there if I needed a bottle to impress a client or give as a gift. Maybe even buy stuff for a little picnic in my own backyard. So why don't you do it?"

"Why does everyone think it's so easy?" My voice was laced with thinly disguised irritation. "For once, my parents were one hundred percent right. I can't do that *and* this. I promised them I'd uphold the family tradition of Canyon Country Mart."

"That's your reason?"

"Oh, there's also the missing employee problem. There've been a lot of technological advancements. Splitting me into two workable clones isn't realistically over the horizon."

"Do it here."

"Where? There's nothing available in the plaza."

"Here, Henry. Turn Canyon Country Mart into your place. Sal retired, right? And you haven't found another deli guy with good prices and high-quality meat. The lunch orders will dry up if you don't figure out something fast. But I've been here a couple of days. You don't love using the meat slicer and fretting over how to keep pickle juice from touching bread without killing the world's forest with endless wax paper. So, do it here. Turn your everything store into what you want."

"Yeah, and what would I call it?"

"Glen. Your menu will be Food plus Glen. Your wine selection will be Wine plus Glen. And so on. I think you could do baskets for the Hollywood Bowl and call them Bowl plus Glen. The possibilities are endless. Inventory's got to be easier not tracking down every pack of bubble gum."

"I already have an off-sale liquor license," I mused.

"See. Easy-peasy." She went over to get the wire and some twine from the tiny hardware section.

She'd just programmed a major change in my life, but was as sanguine about it as if she'd planned a backyard barbecue.

I was quiet because my mind was reeling.

"Could it be that easy?" I asked, not aware it was out loud until Sabrina shifted, turning my way.

"Why not? Back in January, I decided to grab my career by the horns and wrestle it into submission. Look how that turned out...minus the platinum disaster. I was able to get my work on Hollywood's top actresses. No offense, but GLEN isn't curing cancer or world peace. It's taking lemons and making lemonade. In this case, a lemon slash limeade with a mint garnish."

"You know, my grandparents founded that store."

"Are they alive?"

"And well. They retired to Ojai years ago."

"What made them turn over the store to your parents?"

"Happened around the time my mom quit. I think it was their way of making sure my family was taken care of."

"I think it's served its purpose then. Your parents are out. You said you have a brother, right?"

"Evan."

"He's a doctor and doesn't live in the country, so probably not chomping at the bit to take over, right? I think if you called your grandparents, they'd probably give you their blessing—happy that the tradition of supporting the family was being carried on. What makes you think everyone wants it to be a general store?"

What indeed, I thought. Had that stark sense of obligation been in my head? Sure, my parents had been resistant to my changes a few years ago, but I'd stopped pushing. And now that they were gone, surely they didn't expect me to do exactly what they'd done? If that were the case, they could have stayed, found a new deli guy, upgraded the slicers, expanded the bubble gum selection.

Could I start the new year with a store that was my own? My grandparents had founded the store back when movie studios and agriculture were the two major players in the area. My mom had had a foot in one, my father the other. I'd seen the pictures. Back then it had been a farm stand selling local produce up from the Valley to folks who lived on the other side. My mom had come in one day, all huge sunglasses and glamour, and the rest had been history. My grandparents first, and my parents later had worked hard to preserve that history. But maybe now it was time for a new chapter.

"I think my dad has a saw in the garage," I said after we'd gathered up the shears, twine, wire, and food she'd selected, and were back in my car for the short drive across the Mulholland ridgeline toward the place I'd called home my entire life.

"Saw? For what?"

"To make the tree fit."

"In design school, the first lesson was: there is a creative solution to every problem."

"And your fix for this?"

"Definitely not a saw. The Grinch Christmas tree." She nearly sang the last.

"What exactly is that?"

"Do you remember the movie from when we were kids?"

I searched my memory. I'd seen a lot of movies. Probably more than the average kid, given my mom's friends.

"Can't place it," I admitted.

After we got back and I turned on the oven—sure this time, because I did the old-fashioned test of sticking my hand in to make sure it was warm—Sabrina ran to the family room. "Give me a sec." Sabrina left the table and came back with her phone. Fortunately, my house wasn't a complete dead zone and she had at least had two bars of reception. "Here," she said, pressing play on the video viewer. The tree appeared on screen. After a comedic sequence, one last ornament was placed on the tree, bending the tree over.

"That?" I couldn't hide the disbelief that crept into my voice.

"It'll be so cute. We'll do it. Then take a picture and

send it to your family. Better yet, you should post it on your store's social media accounts.

"Social media?"

"Totally another lesson for another day. You can place ads, get great-looking food and wine pictures in front of the audience most likely to patronize your store. It's a bit of work, but once you get it set up, it'll be like second nature. Total win/win."

"What do you need me to do?"

"Drag the tree outside. Get me those shears. Then maybe start a fire and let me know when the food is ready. I'm going to need it."

Chapter Thirteen

SABRINA

"MERRY CHRISTMAS."

I'd opened my eyes to see Henry's sleepy gaze on me. I rolled toward him in his giant California king size so we lay face-to-face. The way he looked at me made all my defenses melt. It was as if he were only seeing me, no one else, and I was the most beautiful woman on Earth. It was singularly baring. Nothing came between us now. He knew the most important things about me, both bad and good, and he was still right here.

My heart cracked open and I wanted to let him in, if only a little bit.

The kiss he placed on my lips was heart-meltingly sweet. It nearly stopped my heart. Sweet and tender were enough to make me feel exposed, vulnerable. When I would have surged forward, gotten down to the nitty-gritty, he kept at it, the stroking of my face and hair and tracing the scar at my chest. I wanted to alternatively shrink away and move toward him.

When his gentle caresses became too much, I pushed him onto his back. Without preamble, I grabbed a condom from his nightstand and lifted the covers, revealing his pulsing cock.

"You don't have to hold back, Henry," I said while rolled the latex over him. Before he could utter a word of either encouragement or protest, I placed a hand in the middle of his chest and notched him with the other. I didn't breathe until I'd enveloped him. Then, and only then, did I let out a hiss of breath.

Even though I was sure he was trying to hold back, he bucked. I met him thrust for thrust. Though his chest was sculpted like a Greek god, he wasn't made of marble. I moved my hands so my fingers were able to drag across his hard little nipples. It was one beat, maybe two, before he lost control and pounded into me. Whether it was my spasms or his that started the cascade, didn't matter. In minutes, our mingled cries filled the air in the room.

When our breathing returned to normal, he pulled the gray duvet over our rapidly cooling bodies.

"I have something I want to give you." He shifted so that he was propped up on an elbow, his head resting on his large hand.

"You already gave me the tickets."

Grabbing both sides of his face, I placed a kiss squarely on his lips. Though I thought myself sated moments ago, I was starting to warm up all over again.

He pulled back, his face serious.

I snaked my hand over the covers and grabbed his still-hard cock through the comforter. "Is this it? Because I so could use more of this."

Gently, he removed my hand. "No, not that. At least right now. I'm being serious."

"I wasn't joking." I scooted up the bed, clutching the covers at my neck. I braced myself for a medical alert bracelet or the like, because what else could he possibly be thinking of?

"Should I let the dog out?" I could hear the quaver in my own voice, but there was something about the intensity of his gaze that was unnerving.

"Sabrina. Sit tight for a minute, please."

I nodded, because what in the hell else was I going to do? Without clothes and my dog leashed, it would be difficult as hell to run out of the house. Though everything in my body was saying that I should run now because things were about to get serious, and I was ready for anything but serious. I heard the bathroom door first, then his front door open and shut, and the click, click of the dog's nails on the steep wooden steps. Henry was taking care of Spencer. There went my dog excuse.

The five minutes that passed may as well have been fifty because each second grated on my raw nerves. When he came back, he was wearing pajama bottoms. He was carrying one of those generic multicolored glossy bags filled with tissue paper. I almost groaned, but held it back.

It didn't take five years of therapy to know that

groaning was not the kind of response one had for a lover. Elation, happiness, and joy would have been far more appropriate, but I couldn't muster up any of those.

Dread was more like it. Sure I'd showed up at his store, admired his biceps, hoped for something more. Hope and want hadn't been that serious.

This.

Henry.

Here.

Was.

Serious, raw, earthy, real and more than I'd imagined it could be.

"I know we haven't been seeing each other long," Henry started as he moved toward the bed, Spencer bringing up the rear, his tail wagging like a metronome.

"Sit," I commanded the dog. "Down." Obediently, the dog lay on a braided rug at the foot of Henry's rustically framed king-size bed.

There was nothing more to do than see what came next. I silently released my breath.

He placed the bag on the nightstand farthest from me, and sat on the bed, cross-legged, facing me.

Henry would lose at poker or any kind of game that required him to hide his feelings. Something akin to love radiated from his eyes, warming them from sky to ocean blue.

Something akin to panic took over me again. Only a fool wouldn't know at least half of what was likely to come.

"I know that we haven't been together long," he started. *Together* ricocheted in my head. "But I think we make a great couple. I mean to say that I think I'm falling in love with you."

"Think?" I asked, because suddenly it was gravely important to know where he stood.

He shook his head, a slow smile widening his lips. "Not think, *know*. I have to admit that I'm a little nervous telling you this so early on. I think I take after my father, though. He knew my mother was the one for him the first time she walked into the store. The rest is history."

Henry's look was expectant. For me, it was like some kind of women's magazine puzzle. Was I supposed to say it back? I liked him a lot, really, but love?

Instead of thinking of something to say, I leaned forward letting the duvet drop from where I'd had it wedged across my chest and under my armpits. Laying both of my hands on his shoulders, I drew him close and kissed him, lightly at first, then with increasing ardor as he responded in kind.

He pulled back an inch or two, his breathing heavy.

"There's something else. Pass me that."

I leaned to the side and retrieved the bag he'd left. Self-conscious once again, I stretched across the bed and found the pajama top I'd worn for all of five seconds the night before, and slipped the cool crinkle gauze tank over my head.

"What's in the bag?"

"All the makings of a great weeklong getaway."

"Go on."

He pulled out a small stack of full-color brochures.

"We'll fly up to San Francisco, then rent a car. I've booked us at a hotel in the Russian River Valley. We'll have a limo drive us to various wineries that make some of the best wines in California. The inn has a Michelin-starred restaurant. There are also some other great places in the valley there. The best part is there's a great hike to the summit of Mount Saint Helena. The brochures say it's about forty-three hundred feet. Ten miles up and back."

"Wow. This sounds incredible. I mean, going to wine country with an actual sommelier would be great."

He smiled. "I have to say I think so myself."

"When would we go? After the Oscars, right? That's March, though. So maybe April or May?"

"I was thinking March. I've gone ahead and made reservations at the bed and breakfast."

"It sounds so lovely, but I can't in March. That's when I'm off to Tanzania. I was pricing tickets yesterday. I'd planned to book the tour, safari, and plane tickets during that quiet week between Christmas and New Years before everything goes back to crazy."

"I thought we'd do this instead. It's something we can do together."

"What are you trying to say?"

"You can't go to Tanzania."

"Why can't I go to Tanzania? They have planes, and guides, and things I want to see and do."

"Because I love you."

The warmth from the post-sex glow that had spread through my body and limbs like warm sap, the warmth from being on the precipice of love that had made me lethargic, turned as cold and hard as amber, leaving me rigid with anger.

"And you won't love me after I come back from Africa? It's an either-or proposition with you. Is that what you're saying?"

"I love you and I don't want you to die."

"What's that phrase?" I mimed searching heaven and earth for the words. "Right. If you love someone, set them free."

"Free to what? Fall down the side of a mountain? Bleed to death before they can get you to a halfway-decent hospital? I don't want to mourn you. I want to be with you —the alive you—*now*. Three months from now and a year from now."

"I'm not going to die. You being there hiking up a tiny Northern California trail with me isn't the thin line between life and death."

"You don't know that."

"You're right. I don't know that. I could die from a mountain lion attack hiking on the trails right around here, or I could get into a car accident, or I could die in a plane crash. I could live my life huddled in my house, free of sharp knives, waiting for the worst or the inevitable. Or I can get out there and fly, and climb, and see the world. I guess the question is whether you're going to do that with me, or am I going to do it alone."

For once, I didn't have any problem expressing my feelings. Because if there was one thing I'd learned, it was that half a life wasn't worth living.

Chapter Fourteen

HENRY

"WHAT WAS YOUR PLAN?" My grandmother rose and stalked across the room toward her wall of framed vintage advertisements. "Wrap her in bubble wrap and keep her in a life-size curio cabinet?"

"That sounds creepy, Grandma." My grandparents had probably spent too much time in retirement watching those psychological horror movies that had been hugely popular a few years back. Grandpa Charles had always been a film buff.

"Keeping a woman locked in a cabinet sounds creepy, but dictating where she can and cannot go doesn't? I watch the news. America isn't Saudi Arabia."

"I wasn't going to revoke her driver's license." I'd never been that kind of guy. Women were equal to men and just as capable, in my book.

"Just her license to live her life free and clear of being dictated to." My grandmother had her arms crossed over her bosom, her word not mine. I hadn't seen her this riled up over something since California wanted to spray area citrus groves with pesticides to ward off the Asian citrus psyllid.

"I love her, though, Grandma. I really do. When she's speaking to me again, I'd love to drive her up to meet you." There hadn't been much speaking after I'd made my ultimatum. She'd packed up her bag and dog and left me with the cute Christmas tree and too much breakfast food.

"Sounds like a lovely girl. Canadian to boot. They're some nice people up there," Grandpa Charles said. It was probably only the second sentence I'd heard from the male half of the grandparent tag team today. "Gonna say, though, it doesn't sound like we're going to meet her unless you apologize."

"For what? Saying I love you? Planning a fabulous trip?"

"You said your trip involved flying to wine country. Doing wine tours. Having wine-paired dinners. Oh, and maybe a quick hiking trip. Honey, I love how you've pursued your passion with wine. We've always supported you in that—even when your parents couldn't see their way clear past you selling beef jerky and soda. But this trip sounds like it's all for you."

"She seemed enthusiastic." I was starting to think I'd been a colossal ass. Wine was *my* thing. Other than that, tacked-on mini hike, I hadn't really considered her needs and desires. Wanting to keep her safe had trumped my common sense.

"She likes you, obviously. But what would be an ideal trip for her?"

"Sabrina wanted an African safari and a hike to the summit of Kilimanjaro."

"Literally worlds away," Grandpa Charles piped in.

I stood and walked to the edge of the patio and did a little turn through their acre of land planted with vegetables, fruit trees, and native plants. Was it for me?

Realization dawned that I'd probably come across like a self-centered prick. Every other word out of my mouth had been wine. She probably wouldn't hate it, might even like it, but varietals and Michelin-starred restaurants were my thing. Not hers.

Damn.

Half an hour later, I wandered back into their house just as my grandfather was setting dinner on the table. Chicken-fried steak and fried okra. I couldn't eat like this every day, but I didn't turn it down, either. My grandparents had shed most of their own parents' native Oklahoma culture, but not the food when it was time for family get-togethers.

"I came here for another reason," I said after I'd taken my empty dinner plate to the kitchen and brought back some kind of fruit cobbler. I couldn't tell quite what it was under the dough. Probably some combo of the apples and quince that grew in my grandparents' garden, I guessed.

"What's that, Henry? We told you we don't need gifts. We have everything we could ever need in these few square feet."

"Although always seeing more of you is a gift," my grandma said with one of those smiles that let me know she wasn't at all angry with me, despite her earlier words.

I ushered them to the patio with the incentive that I'd make them coffees. I got the espresso machine I'd bought them years ago down from a dusty shelf in the pantry, cleaned it off and made them a couple of decaf cappuccinos. Once I set the drinks and Christmas gift of tuiles on the crackle glass surface, I pulled up a chair and looked at each of them.

"It's about the shop."

"I can't believe that Chester and Jill up and left. I thought they'd die there."

"They probably said the same about you, Gramps."

"Touché. Hey, Victoria. Can you get that blue and gold album off the top of the TV shelf?"

A few minutes later, my grandmother came out holding the album like it was an antique family bible. Inwardly, I groaned.

Like I'd done when my brother, Evan, and I had sat at a similar table and taken out the same album when our grandparents had been in Los Angeles, I settled in for a long evening.

My grandfather's arthritic fingers opened the album slowly, like a movie director building up tension. The first page was as familiar to me as my own face.

It was a single framed photograph of my grandfather and grandmother, both looking impossibly young, standing in front of a sold sign perched on the store's porch. The succeeding pages were like a walk through post-World War Two history. Theirs was the only store on the hill. Then in the late fifties, there were pictures of the construction, other stores growing up around theirs, first in wood, then later in smooth, modern stucco.

The inside of the store changed as well, with most dry goods in cardboard while drinks were in glass. I could scarcely imagine how heavy deliveries would have been back then. Now nearly everything was in thin cardboard, plastic, or cellophane.

There was a lot of "remember this" and "fancy that" back and forth between my grandparents as they turned the pages. In the latter half of the book, my mom appeared. First as a young movie star, then later as a mom with first Evan, then with both me and my brother crowded on her lap. The store certainly had provided a living for three generations of Barnhills.

The little walk down memory lane did two things. It made me a little less hostile toward the place that was, in a sense, holding me hostage. It also made me nervous with what I was about to announce.

Gramps turned the last page, which was a close-up of the newest Canyon Country Mart sign my parents had updated a few years ago, then Gramps closed the book with a long sigh.

"What did you come to say, young one?"

My confidence, buoyed by Sabrina's unchecked enthusiasm earlier, fled. I fiddled with the cover of the album for a few seconds before my grandfather spoke again.

"You want to close the store, don't you? Do your own thing?"

"No, no. That's not it at all," I protested, then relented. "Well, that's partially it." I took a deep breath and thought of how much faith Sabrina had in my ability to make a go of a wine and gourmet food shop.

"First, I want to change the name."

"Oh, it's always been Canyon Country Mart," my grandmother said, pulling at the neck of her short-sleeved blouse as if she had pearls at her neck that needed clutching.

"I know, but we're in a new century and a lot of things have changed." I parroted Sabrina's words.

"What do you want to call it?" Gramps asked.

"Glen," I said.

"How will people know what you sell there? Maybe Glen Market?" Grandma said.

"There's more. I..." I hesitated only a moment. I needed to change the way I was speaking. I was a grown man, not a child asking permission. Didn't the saying go that it was easier to ask forgiveness or something like that? "I'm going to change what I sell there. It's going to be wine and gourmet food."

"No lunch?" my grandpa asked.

"Nope, no lunch." My voice was firm, confident. "We'll do specialty food baskets to order. Next summer, we'll supply food and wine for Once Upon a Canyon Night over at Tree People, as well as baskets for the Holly-wood Bowl. There's a higher profit margin per item than on lunch deli sandwiches. Between expanding craft services and commissaries, and roaming food trucks, our hold on lunch was slipping. Oh, and Sal retired, by the way."

"Oh, honey, remember when we first met Sal?" My grandmother's eyes danced in delight. "He was a young gun back then."

"Talked me out of my supplier. He had good prices and on-time delivery. Takes time to develop those kinds of relationships."

"I'm working on some of my own. Met quite a few importers when I was in France and Italy. I hope to meet more from Germany and maybe even Portugal. They have some very interesting things going on there."

"Sounds like you have it all figured out," my grandmother said. Her voice sounded a little put out.

"I love you guys, and I am immensely grateful for what you started and what Mom and Dad built. But it's time to go my own way on this. I have to keep up with what consumers today want. They can get sandwiches, soda, cigarettes, and gum where they buy their gas now. It's the more obscure items that people are clamoring for. Home prices are stratospheric in the Hills, so it's a more well-heeled and discriminating buyer these days."

While the sun set over the ocean, I pulled out my tablet and showed them the logo that Sabrina had designed, as well as the first draft of my business plan.

"Are you planning to ask the bank for a loan?"

I nodded. This is where it got sticky, but I was

prepared for the question. "Interest rates are favorable. If I'm not willing to bet on myself, then no one will be. I need the money for renovations and at least two full-time employees until we can become profitable. I'm giving it at least three years."

My grandparents looked at each other, and I wondered if they were going to try to nip the whole thing in the bud. They were the landowners, and though I had no real leasing expenses, they could say no.

"Henry, I think we need to talk about ownership structure."

My head spun as the conversation took an unexpected turn. "What do you mean?"

"It's time we talk about the plaza."

I squinted in the quickly waning twilight, trying to figure out what in the heck they were getting at.

"You know that we've always owned the land the store was built on, right? It's what made us more successful than a lot of storeowners in Los Angeles. We had no landlord to jack up the rent and make our profits unstable."

I nodded. I'd always known that part. Flipping through the album minutes before had not been the first time I'd seen my grandparents posing next to that sold sign. It was kind of an iconic picture in our family's history.

"It's a bit more than that. We own the land under the entire plaza."

"Wait, the other people pay money to an LLC. Kenton, I think." It had come up at occasional meetings about our shared facilities. I'd never mentioned that my parents weren't paying rent, and the other tenants never asked.

I was looking between them when the connection fell on me like a ton of bricks. Kenton was the Panhandle town they'd emigrated from. I'd heard some distant stories about it, but not many, as my grandparents had come to the area as babies.

"We're Kenton, Henry." My grandmother confirmed my suspicions.

"Why didn't Mom and Dad ever tell us?"

"It wasn't theirs to tell."

I made rough calculations based on my limited knowledge of rents in the plaza. My modest-living grandparents were raking in at least a million a year. Those kinds of numbers nearly made my head explode.

"We've always planned to leave that to you and Evan. William died before he could have any kids."

William had been my father's brother. He'd died of cancer back before survival rates and treatments had advanced to where they were today.

"We'll have to talk to the lawyers and accountants to make sure this is sound, but we'll start paying you and Evan a portion of the monthly proceeds, maybe fifteen percent each, offset by your percentage after we sign the land over to you lock, stock, and barrel. The rest will stay in the trust, which you and your brother will split when that time comes."

"You guys have a long life ahead of you," I blurted out. I hated to think about what life would be like after they were gone. For a long time, they'd been the backbone of my family. Here I was now, seeking their counsel and support like I'd done countless times over the years.

"Researchers haven't found the gene for immortality yet, my boy."

"Bottom line is that you're not opposed then?" I asked, my head spinning from the turnaround of events.

"Not our monkey, not our circus, Henry. Sounds like you have a good plan, and a good potential lifetime partner in your smart lady friend. We want you to be happy. Now, get me a second serving of that dessert, so we can celebrate."

I rose to do their bidding, but I stopped when my grandmother laid a hand on my arm.

"Money and work aren't everything. We're going to be thrilled to go to your grand opening, but until then you need to make sure you make love the most important priority. You hear me?"

I nodded. I heard my grandmother loud and clear.

Chapter Fifteen

FOR THE TEN THOUSANDTH TIME, I wiped my palms on my black skinny jeans, then straightened my black cashmere turtleneck. When I'd made the decision to leave Vancouver and seek my fortune in Hollywood like so many Canadians before me, I'd imagined it a bit more glamorous.

Standing in a freezing-cold conference room while I was alternately sweating and had chills was the least thrilling thing I could have imagined. I sat down in one of the high-backed leather chairs and turned my back to the view of the Hollywood sign nestled among the hills she called home. Instead, I reorganized all that I'd brought, rearranging it on the conference table one more time.

"Are you okay being here, helping me?" I asked Mona.

"Sure, absolutely," my neighbor said, not jiggling with nerves like I was. The woman who sometimes helped me with presentations was away for the holidays like most sane non-Angelenos were.

"I don't want you to meet them later somewhere and not have them buy your art because they thought you were someone's assistant."

"If being someone's assistant were a bar to employment, ninety-nine percent of this town would be unemployed. Everyone starts somewhere in this city. Sometimes Los Angeles is a pretty diplomatic place. Trust me, if any one of these people are at my next show downtown, they'll truly not remember me, or they'll have the grace to pretend they don't. No worries."

My friend and neighbor was an odd one. Half the time she was full of snark and dragging one tattooed boyfriend or another around. The other half of the time, she acted like she was from some elite San Francisco or Philadelphia family and had attended finishing school, or whatever the modern equivalent of that would have been. It didn't much matter who Mona was today. I was extremely grateful for the help.

"Okay, I'll put it out of my mind. Now can you help me get these cases just so, and tell me again which lights are which."

Mona stood and gripped my shoulders hard. That one moment did more to restore my sanity than anything else in the last half hour. "Sliders are spotlights. Switches are fluorescent."

We worked efficiently to get everything just right. Then we sat. My chair jiggled with my leg.

"Stop it." Mona closed her kohl-stained lids and rubbed each index and middle finger along her temples. "I see success in your future," she intoned, doing her best Carnac the Magnificent imitation.

That little bit of theater made me laugh and released some of my pent-up tension.

I rose to my feet again when the door opened and a whole group of people filed in. Among them was a newly minted agent, Matt Ridenour, who worked for one of the guys with his name on the building. I'd met Matt years ago when we were both new to Los Angeles and went to the kind of mixers new residents frequented. Now Matt was an assistant agent to the guy who repped doyenne Kimberly Welch, and he was the main agent for the up-and-coming Heidi Dunn. Various public relations reps and managers filled out the room.

Done sitting at home playing the victim, I rose and started to speak so I could take control of the meeting. Experience had taught me that if I didn't, it would become a giant clusterfuck and I'd be out of a job faster than I could say self-destructing jewelry. In order to achieve the goals I'd set for myself a year earlier, I needed the rest of this awards season to go off without a hitch.

"Ladies and gentlemen," I started after I'd introduced Mona. Then I flipped the latches and popped open the two portable display cases. The brown leather opened on a diagonal to reveal black velvet pendant stands. I'd pasted a headshot of each actress in the corresponding box.

Several of the women gasped and the men's eyes

widened. Hundreds of thousands of dollars' worth of glittering stones did that to people.

It never failed.

"These are the completed necklaces and matching earrings," I said. I gestured to my right. "This is for Kimberly Welch, diamonds in platinum. The other single pear-shaped or teardrop stone, this ten-carat opal, is for Heidi Dunn. You'll see that I've worked diamonds, opals, and crystals into the chain for minimum weight and maximum sparkle. I've consulted with both dress designers to complete a design that will complement, while making your clients stand out from the crowd on the red carpet."

Drawing in a deep breath, I prepared to get out in front of the questions I knew they'd have.

"I'm sure you're aware of the difficulties that have accompanied my work for Gemma Hart and Mina Foy in the last months. I'm happy to say that the problem's been fixed entirely. It was a metal contamination problem. I've worked in a nearly hermetically sealed room for the last two weeks to get these finished. I came here in good faith to assure you I can deliver on what was promised."

I pointed to Mona, the cue for my friend to stand. Shucking a black leather motorcycle jacket, Mona revealed an off-the-shoulder turquoise blouse the same color as Kimberly Welch's gown. I then pointed to another woman in the room, who was conveniently wearing a V-neck top.

"Can you ladies please take off your jewelry and come here?"

The women obeyed and I carefully fastened the ambitious branching design for Kimberly Welch to Mona, and the elaborate pendant for Heidi Dunn to the other.

"Mona Love," Matt asked as he spun in his chair lazily. "Have I seen you somewhere before?"

Mona stiffened just as I was working the clasp. I nearly dropped the necklace to the floor.

"I'm sure we haven't met." Mona was shifting around nervously, and not at all still which would have made fastening the tiny clasp much easier.

"You kind of remind me of this girl I once knew, Emmaline Pad...Padgett." He snapped his fingers.

"Nope. Mona Love. I'm a visual artist helping out a friend today."

With my friend's jerky movements, it took me more than a second to get the necklace clasped, but I finally did. Asking the other woman to turn and lift her blonde hair, I affixed the second necklace. Releasing another breath, I stepped back from the volunteers.

"Ladies, can you please take a walk around the room like you normally would? Also, try pulling at the jewelry to see if there are any weak spots."

Again, they followed my direction, and I tried not to feel like a magician who was about to present some sleight of hand or a game-show model announcing the grand prize.

Camera phones rose as a couple of people took pictures. I was glad I'd mucked with the lighting before they'd stepped in. No one had noticed in the slightly dimmed room that the halogens were on full blast, while the fluorescent lights were off.

"Hey," one of the PR women shouted. "You cannot share before the show. Like the dress, this has to be a secret. We'll leak the cost information and designer, but will not have any pictures go out. You understand?"

One of the phone-wielding assistants nodded, suitably cowed. I didn't care either way. Early leaking would stir up excitement. Or a reveal on the carpet would allow for a big splash. My body nearly doubled over with relief. If they were debating when to release information, then I had them. Alternative designers or the usual corporate jewelers were off the table.

"If you guys can cut a check today," I said. "I'm happy to leave these here. Otherwise, I'll need to take these back to my studio and arrange for delivery later."

Matt shot a look to the only man in a suit, obviously his own assistant, who jumped up and ran out of the room. A few minutes later, the assistant was back with a check for the full amount. I would save my sigh of relief and hoots of joy until I was well out of earshot of the suits.

After the room cleared out, half the people already on their phones putting out celebrity fires, I fell to my knees. I resisted the urge to line up my hands in prayer and praise God for the small success I'd just had.

"You were a champ. Ballsy the way you asked for the money like that."

"I needed them to have no way to back out," I said. "Came to me at the last minute. Something Henry said about going for it."

I packed up the now empty cases and slipped the

check into my wallet and tucked the leather safely inside my purse. It wasn't diamonds I was carrying, but I needed to guard it nonetheless. Make sure I got that huge check to the bank as soon as possible to pay back my suppliers.

"Speaking of Henry..." Mona shrugged on her jacket. My friend went from tender to tough in a heartbeat.

"I wasn't speaking of Henry." I slipped on my own coat and we headed toward the elevators.

Mona pushed the down button about a thousand times. "Why not?"

"I have nothing more to say about it. Really, I don't." I'd already done this battle with my parents. It was half of what had propelled me south. I did not plan to watch the rest of the world and my life go by from a sickbed.

"So what? A guy tells you he loves you, takes your advice about his store, and you don't talk to him? That makes zero sense. I mean, I'm a player, and what you're doing doesn't even follow any rules of any game I've ever heard of."

After we got to the underground parking, I popped the trunk and stuffed everything in. "I'm not playing any game, Mona. I like Henry. Might even love him. But he can't decide where I go and what I do."

"The heart thing?" Mona asked as she got into the passenger seat.

"The heart thing." I got in and started the small car. Despite the winter-cool weather, I left the top down. Maybe the air would clear my head of any idea of bowing to Henry's unreasonable demands. Because despite what my mind knew was best, my body still craved his kisses and his touch. My heart, my heart was a whole other matter.

"You could have told me. I'm the very definition of unshakeable." My friend *was* pretty solid. But the words "heart surgery" were like the word "cancer." Mention either of the two and people lost their grip on reason pretty quickly.

"I'd love to see you in an earthquake," I said as I cleared Sunset Boulevard and started my way up the hill.

"You're losing me, maze mind."

"Do you know why I told him?"

Mona shook her head, her unbound black hair whipped by the wind.

"Because he was going to see me naked. When you strip down for a guy for the first time, it's usually a good idea to explain the nine-inch scar bisecting your chest."

"Nine inches?"

"Twenty-two centimeters."

"Jesus," Mona breathed.

"He said it didn't freak him out. Then..."

"Let me guess? He freaked out."

"Bingo." I beat my hand on the steering wheel in tempo with the word.

"Because you cut your finger helping him with his lunch rush."

"He thinks because it took a minute to stop my finger from bleeding that I'm going to die hiking Kilimanjaro."

"You're still going to do that?" I had to appreciate that Mona didn't put that "fear of God" sound in her voice.

"After this meeting, I've reached nearly every last one of my near-term goals. I don't want to stop because a guy lets fear rule his life. I mean, he's been toiling in that shop instead of stepping away to do what he wants. Then his parents drop the store in his lap and he still hesitates. You know what I learned from open-heart surgery?"

"What?"

"That courage is overcoming fear. That I have one life and I'm not going to spend it in bubble wrap. I got a second chance with the valve. A hundred years ago, I'd have died. Now, I want to live."

"Preach it, sister." Mona threw up her hands like we were on the downward slope of a roller coaster.

We high-fived. When I turned my attention back to the road, I had to swerve to correct myself and get back in my own lane.

"Well, let me at least get us home alive and intact, otherwise I won't get any farther than the morgue of Saint Joseph's."

We both let our hair fly all the way home.

With the substantial check in my lockbox for safekeeping, I knew it was time to do a good turn for someone else, pay it forward. So I fished through the junk jar downstairs for the cameo. Once and for all, I was going to attack the problem of contacting former owners and getting the antique to where it belonged.

But it wasn't there.

Frustrated, I looked at Spencer. He just gave me his doggy-jowled face, but had no answers. I tore upstairs to my studio. Hadn't I been looking at it up there with Mona or Henry a couple of weeks ago? I searched from corner to corner, stem to stern, and no damned cameo.

I gave up and pulled out canned and dry food for the dog. I mixed, then put the bowl down on the floor. While he ate, I poked around with the broom from the tall cabinet where I kept cleaning supplies. But nothing.

I shook off the superstitious feeling that was settling on my shoulders. The feeling that the cameo was somehow related to Henry and it was missing now that he was MIA. Instead of dwelling, I gathered my resolve and found my laptop.

My first e-mail was to my travel agent. Then I opened my browser and started to fill up my virtual shopping cart from my favorite outdoor and travel gear store. Excitement burbled through my chest, setting off the faint clicking of my valve. I was ready for my next adventure, and if I had to do it alone, then so be it.

Chapter Sixteen

"I'D TAKE you if I could," I said to my friend Mona, "but I only got one."

Case in point, I took the single gold-embossed ticket from the Hollywood Foreign Press Association and brandished it before the mirror.

"Honey, you don't need a date to the most fabulous event in town this weekend. Just drink up and enjoy."

I turned this way and that, admiring the borrowed gown. "Where did you get this fabulous dress from?"

"A girl can't reveal her sources. I'm just glad it fits."

And fit it did. I felt like a princess in the silk creation. Standing in the full-length mirror, admiring myself, was far closer to my vision of life in Los Angeles than the unglamorous nature of daily life.

"It's like I'm Cinderella, with the mystery ticket that arrived by messenger, and the mystery dress that fits like a glove that you were able to procure. Will a white pumpkin-shaped limo arrive in half hour?"

"I'm pretty sure the car service will send a boring old black luxury car. And it won't turn into a pumpkin at midnight."

I looked at myself again, twirling and looking over my shoulder to see if my bum looked big. The off-the-shoulder copper gown fit like it was custom made. The swoop up to one shoulder revealed as much skin as it covered. I didn't thank my friend outright, but I was thrilled the fabric had covered my scar, and not in a way that made it look like I was stepping out of prim Victorian England.

Despite how childish it seemed, I twirled and watched the light as chiffon layers lifted and landed back on my bedroom floor with grace.

"Is this jewelry okay?" I extended her arms toward Mona.

Ironic that I didn't have a ton of jewelry on hand. I hadn't made many pieces for myself in years, not since I'd been in my twenties and amazed at my own skills. But none of those various beaded pieces were a fit for the elegant silk. Except for a giant yellow topaz cocktail ring and a hammered gold cuff on my right wrist, I was unadorned. I wasn't there to show off, though, but to see my creations in person. It was going to be elegant enough so that I didn't get laughed out of the Beverly Hilton.

"You look beautiful." Mona's face held no hint of amusement or scorn both regular features on her face.

"It's your makeup." I looked at the face I'd had all my

life, contoured and glammed up to make me look like a movie star who belonged on the red carpet. "Mona, you're a woman of many more talents than I knew."

"Just because I turn garbage into art, doesn't mean I don't know my way around a smoky eye and a glossy lip. Look how my skills came in handy."

I blotted my lips one last time and picked up the purse I'd bought last minute at Bloomingdales, thankfully open and fully staffed on a Sunday. The tiny gold Halston clutch was fitted with lipstick, my phone—set to vibrate— and the keys to get me back into my house when the coach turned into a pumpkin.

"Thanks for your offer to watch Spencer, but he'll be fine. Drinks start at half past two in the afternoon. I figure I'll be home by ten at the very latest. If you give him his kibble at six and let him out to do his business, he should be okay until I get home."

It was only for a second, but I swore I saw a secret Mona Lisa-type smile on my friend's face. But when I turned from the mirror to face Mona directly, the smile had disappeared, or more than likely had never been there.

The doorbell sounded at the same time my phone buzzed in my bag. I checked the straps on my three-inch heels one last time, then carefully bunched the dress fabric in my hand and descended the stairs.

"It's white." I felt a shiver shake my body as I stepped through my front gate. The "car" that was waiting for me was a pearl-white limo, its middle windows covered by curtains that bordered on mauve. Either this was all a little creepy or I was acting like a kid spooked by scary campfire stories. Chalking up the feeling in my stomach to nerves, I stepped into the open back door as the driver stood by.

"Ma'am." He tipped his head and closed the door as soon as all of my dress was inside with me.

As the car glided from the curb, I looked at the insides. A couple of bottles of water imported from far-flung places on Earth sat in a little holder across from my seat. When I looked around to see what else was stocked in the rolling coach, I noticed a small black box tied with coppery-brown ribbon. The ribbon was nearly the same color as my dress.

I nearly knocked on the window between me and the driver to get permission to open it, but pulled at the small card tied to the ribbon instead. It didn't come loose, but I was able to flip it over. "For Sabrina Lynch" was all it said. No from, no signature.

This all had to be the doing of Eminence, the talent agency repping Welch and Dunn. Slipping off the ribbon, I lifted the top of the box from the bottom.

I nearly screamed when I saw what was inside.

It was "my" cameo. At least I thought it was the one from my house. I flipped it over and there it was, that confounding engraving:

> *Love has this jet to which she clings*
> *With ivory and circling locks about*
> *Bone within silver to cast fear out*
> *Love once found has need of no such thing*
> *Set it free on a pair of dauntless wings*

WITH SHAKING HANDS, I lifted the chain and unclasped the lobster claw. Not touching a single strand of my updo, I closed it. It fit perfectly, nestled where the dress cut away.

Less than fifteen minutes later, the limo was pulling up behind a long line of black cars. I pressed the button most likely to lower the panel between me and the driver. Fortunately, it worked on the first try.

"Do I get out here?"

"My instructions, Ms. Lynch, were to deliver you to the red carpet."

The red carpet. Was I expected to walk down it like I was a celebrity? Somehow, I'd thought there was going to be a back door for someone of my caliber, not the grand front entrance on Wilshire Boulevard.

The wait in the limo line was longer than the drive. But before I'd girded what needed girding and had mustered all the courage in the world, the car glided to a stop, and the driver was opening the door. Doing my best lift of my legs and swivel of my butt, I turned and placed both sandal-clad feet on the ground.

But instead of the dark gray-suited driver, there was an entirely different man who extended his hand.

"Henry!"

"Ms. Lynch," he said, tenderly grasping my hand in his. He lifted and I ducked my head and stood.

"Oh my God, what are you doing here?"

"I'm here to escort you, as your date, to the Golden Globe awards...if you'll have me."

"Of course I'll have you." I'd wanted him to let me live my life, not leave it. There was more to say. Much more. But this wasn't the time nor place. There would be days, week, and months, if not years, for us to smooth out the wrinkles of our relationship.

I followed his lead and tucked my forearm in the crook of his elbow. As we took mincing steps through the throng of reporters, I took him in. All of him. The tuxedo he wore had a modern cut, while being classic at the same time, and fitted him like a second skin. His broad shoulders and narrow waist were emphasized. The silk bow tie knotted at the throat of his perfectly starched white shirt. My heart skipped a beat, then did a little dance inside my chest. This gorgeous, gorgeous man was here for me and me alone. It made all that had come before forgivable—almost.

The walk to the doors was like some kind of processional, reminding me of my high school prom. Any moment, I expected a photo booth to show up. At least I would look better in any picture taken today than that one from more than a decade past.

Dazed and confused was the only way to describe the feeling of walking a carpet I'd only seen on television. I almost tripped when Henry's hand slipped from mine. Before I could turn to see what had delayed him, the crowd grew oddly quiet, like a faucet of sound had been turned off. Whirling, I looked to find Henry on bended knee.

What in the hell was he doing? We hadn't known each

other long enough to propose marriage. Had he lost his mind altogether?

Undaunted by what must have been a look of shock on my face, he cleared his throat.

"Sabrina Lynch, I love you and want to spend the month of March with you."

"March?" I couldn't stop myself from blurting.

From his pocket, he extracted a small velvet box. With his other hand, he unhinged it. More than a dozen heads leaned in to see what was inside. I craned my neck also for a look.

It was a small brass lock.

For a long second, I just stared, wondering if this was some kind of dream or nightmare, because my head could make sense of none of it. If my mind was a maze, like Mona often said, then it was at a dead end.

"It's a backpack lock," he said, lifting it and two keys from the box.

Backpack lock?

"Will you hike Kilimanjaro with me?"

The gasp of surprise had to be mine. The murmurs of wonder, everyone else.

"Yes, Henry Barnhill, I'd love to go to Tanzania with you!"

Despite my promise to myself not to wreck my makeup, hair, or dress in the first hour, I threw my arms around him as he stood. His strong arms banded around my waist and he twirled me in the air. A whoop went up from the crowd of onlookers as I got the best kiss of my life.

Epilogue

SABRINA

I SIPPED at the champagne offered and tried not to feel out of place in the first-class lounge of the international terminal at LAX. If Canadians ran the world, there would probably be no such thing as first class. I glanced around the room with its strategically placed lighting and whisper-quiet wait staff and concluded that first class wasn't half bad.

"How did you manage this upgrade?" I asked my boyfriend of the last few months. I swept my feet half under my bum getting comfortable on the plush sofa. Might as well enjoy it.

Henry's long, lean body filled the leather club chair, his legs and feet extended in front of him. He drained his flute—he'd chosen a mimosa—and carefully placed it on the glass top table in front of us.

"Luck?"

The half smile playing around his gorgeous lips told me there wasn't a lot of truth in that.

I sipped again, the bubbles tickling my nose. I tilted my head a little to the side and fixed him with a semi-serious stare.

His smile was full. He reached across the small table and took my free hand in his. I felt a little lightheaded at his touch or the alcohol or both.

"It's a gift from my grandmother," he said. "She waited until this morning to tell me because she knew you'd find a way to weasel out of this gift she wanted to give you."

I didn't give truth to that. His grandma was right. Gracious acceptance of the generosity of others was something I was working on. Being humble was one thing, but not letting other people do for you was another.

I was learning that being self sufficient didn't mean not accepting the help and love from others. I'd started trying this out with my parents and my relationship with them was better for it. They trusted me to make the right decisions. I trusted that their concern was out of love and not an attempt to control me.

"Aw. That's lovely. I really enjoyed meeting them. I wished we could have spent more than a weekend in Ojai." Henry's grandparents were everything Henry was, kind, warm, generous, and accepting.

"They loved you too. They were really keen on your ideas for the store."

"I'm so glad Glen all went over well—the Food plus

Glen and Wine plus Glen ideas. I was so worried they'd think I was stepping all over their legacy."

"They've always been forward looking. It's that boldness that made them take a risk on buying that property when Los Angeles was a Western outpost before it became what it is now."

I sat forward a bit. Most days I was as excited about the future of the store as Henry.

"And they're okay overseeing the renovations while we're gone?" I asked.

"They probably wouldn't admit it, but I'm pretty sure Grandpa doesn't mind too much about being pulled out of retirement for this."

"It'll be amazing to see it all in place when we get back. I'm super excited that you get to have your wine store."

"It wouldn't have been possible without you." Henry squeezed my hand. "I was so set on West Hollywood when this perfect opportunity was right under my nose."

"Have your mom and dad come around yet?" There'd been a lot of raised voices and long silences during Henry's video calls to them.

"They will. It's funny that my mom who came into the family business was more attached to it than dad."

From what I could gather, Chuck Barnhill had been his usual easygoing and affable self while his mom had turned up the drama.

"Are they coming back to Los Angeles?" I knew Henry missed his folks, but I kind of wanted them to see the store when it was up and running and successful so they couldn't derail what Henry was destined to do.

"Not for a couple of months at least. Mom's doing yoga teacher training. Dad's catching up on all the books and movies that he'd missed when he worked nights and weekends."

Relieved that he'd get a chance to see Glen come into being, I let go of his hand and leaned into the leather and drained the bubbly. The intercom squawked and I looked up toward the ceiling listening.

"KLM flight six zero two to Amsterdam Schiphol is now boarding," the disembodied voice started. "Please make your way to the concourse and your gate."

"That's us," I said, popping up immediately. I placed my right hand over my heart. It was beating quickly. Henry stood and placed his large hand over mine.

"You okay?" he asked, his voice just above a whisper.

Grateful at his discretion, I answered, "I haven't been this nervous since the last few awards ceremonies."

"Everything went off without a hitch though. You have more commissions than you ever have."

"I know. It's just that I'm happy, I guess. I have everything I've ever wanted. And I'm going to climb a huge mountain. What was I thinking? Who climbs mountains?"

"You do, Sabrina. You go for your dreams with full-hearted determination."

The way he looked at me was like a balm. I was brave because I had to be. Because I'd learned that life could throw a girl one heck of a curveball, and it was better to catch it than duck. I turned my palm outward and intertwined my fingers with Henry's once again.

"I love you, Henry Barnhill, soon-to-be mountain hiker."

"I love you, Sabrina Lynch. You're the bravest woman in the world and I can't wait to go on this adventure called life with you."

When Sabrina Met Henry

Sabrina: I used to go to Corey's Discount Pet Center.

Henry: To buy dog food for Spencer?

Sabrina: And to spy on you.

Henry: You noticed me?

Sabrina: Who didn't notice you. The hot young son of Chester Barnhill. With biceps that make you want to shout "hallelujah!"

Henry: You like my arms? (laughing quietly) Yeah, you like my arms...

Sabrina: Hefting boxes and stocking shelves at Canyon Country Mart did you proud.

Henry: I may have sold you food and wine. More than you needed just so I could keep talking to you.

Sabrina: And I may have bought all that food to keep talking to you. It's too bad I got too tongue-tied to ask you for coffee and when I think I finally worked up the courage, well, then you disappeared for months at a time.

Henry: (shrugging) Sommelier training took me all over the world.

Sabrina: Ultimately, it was a little cameo that brought us together.

Henry: You really believe that? I vote for Spencer having brought us together.

Sabrina: My dog?

Henry: He literally wrapped me up in his leash and brought me to my knees before you.

Sabrina: (grabbing Henry's hand in mine) Whether it was the cameo or the dog, I don't know. But I'm glad we finally found each other.

Henry: You bring out the best in me.

Sabrina: Same here...

Sometimes Good Girls do Bad Things

From up here on stage, I can see her. Even with her First Lady hair and Sunday school shoes, I can't take my eyes off of her.

The music starts. I swing my hips to the thumping bass. Oh, so slowly I slip one button through a hole, then another, then another. I ease the black silk from my shoulders and toss it right toward her.

I watch her pale glossy lips form a big 'O' before she catches it like a major league baller. The flashing lights blind me. Between beats, I can see her blue eyes zeroed in below my waist.

I know what she wants. I give it to her. With a zip and

a tug, the leather pants join the rest of my clothes. In my skin tight briefs, I dance just for her. With the last chord of the song, the stage goes dark.

I know when the lights come up again, another guy will be dancing in my place because this is my last time. I'm not doing this ever again. It's too bad I didn't get her name. I really liked that shirt. But not enough to go back and claim it.

If she wants me bad enough, she'll have to find me.

About the Author

I write crazy, beautiful love stories because I believe story-telling is magic. I love complicated heroines with secrets, strong heroes who fall hard, and a long winding road to happily ever after. When I'm not writing, I love to travel to witness the diverse tapestry of humanity, photograph the beauty of the world, visit museums, and watch live theater. I live in West Hollywood, California ten miles from the nearest airport.

♥

I haven't found my own happily ever after, but I'm not done trying. This year I'm going to go on fifty first dates.

Join me as I try to find my Mr. Right or maybe Mr. Right Now. #50firstdates #joliemoore #crazybeautifullove

joliemoore.com/50firstdates/

- facebook.com/xojoliemoore
- twitter.com/xojoliemoore
- instagram.com/xojoliemoore
- pinterest.com/xojoliemoore
- amazon.com/author/xojoliemoore
- goodreads.com/xojoliemoore